~ *You're going in?* inquired his brain.

~ *Yes.*

~ *You know what Labyrinth means, don't you?*

~ *It's like a maze.*

~ *No. Maze suggests summer afternoons and cucumber sandwiches and after half an hour of amusing fun you come out again and perhaps play croquet on the lawn. Labyrinth suggests dark tunnels underground designed to lose you forever, until the next unfortunate tumbles in and finds your bones. I was very quiet with the dinosaurs and you hardly heard me at all with those weird men with hot pokers and you know how I feel about pain. But can we skip this?*

~ *And just leave Gen in here?*

~ *Well, that's my point,* said his brain. *I don't know why you think she's going to be somewhere like this. Quincy is a criminal mastermind. He'd send her to the last place any of you would ever look. These are the first places you're going to look. Why not go straight to the last place?*

Also by James Valentine

Jumpman Rule 1: Don't Touch Anything

TIMEMASTER

JUMPMAN®

RULE 2
DON'T EVEN
THINK
ABOUT IT!

JAMES · VALENTINE

CORGI BOOKS

JUMPMAN RULE TWO
A CORGI BOOK 0552 55059 0

Published in Great Britain by Corgi Books,
an imprint of Random House Children's Books

First published in Australia by Random House Australia Pty Ltd, 2003
This edition published 2005

1 3 5 7 9 10 8 6 4 2

Set in MetaPlusBook 10.5/16pt

Corgi Books are published by
Random House Children's Books,
61-63 Uxbridge Road, London W5 5SA,
a division of The Random House Group Ltd,
in Australia by Random House Australia (Pty) Ltd,
20 Alfred Street, Milsons Point, Sydney, NSW 2061, Australia,
in New Zealand by Random House New Zealand Ltd,
18 Poland Road, Glenfield, Auckland 10, New Zealand,
and in South Africa by Random House (Pty) Ltd,
Endulini, 5A Jubilee Road, Parktown 2193, South Africa

THE RANDOM HOUSE GROUP Limited Reg. No. 954009

A CIP catalogue record for this book is available from the British Library.

Printed and bound in Great Britain by Cox & Wyman ltd, Reading, Berkshire.

For Ruby

ZONE ► TimeMaster Museum
EXHIBIT ► 2154541s-367-3145457/PLAQUE
VIEW ► Quote from Quincy Carter One's
submission to the First United Planets
Subcommittee on TimeTravel

PEOPLE GET TOO FOCUSED ON THE PROBLEM
OF MOVING A HUMAN BODY THROUGH TIME.
THAT IS NOT THE PROBLEM. THE PROBLEM IS
MOVING A SINGLE ATOM THROUGH TIME.
ONCE WE CAN MOVE A SINGLE ATOM
THROUGH TIME, THE PROBLEM IS SOLVED.
TO MOVE A HUMAN BODY WE JUST HAVE
TO DO WHAT WE DO WITH A SINGLE ATOM
A TRILLION TIMES OVER. SIMULTANEOUSLY.

QUINCY CARTER ONE

chapter one
Time Out

 PRESENT NOW

FRIDAY NIGHT ▲ EARLY MIL 3

Jules hadn't known you could sweat so much from the palms of your hands.

Under your arms, on top of your head, sure, but this was like someone had just installed a sprinkler system beneath his fingers. Could he wipe them again? But where? Couldn't wipe them on his clothes and he'd already wiped them twice on the cinema seat. Do it again and Gen'd be sure to notice. But here they were a third of the way into the movie and he hadn't even tried to hold her hand.

Why don't I just forget about it and enjoy the movie? Jules thought.

~ *I wish you would*, sighed his brain. *Do you want to know what's happened so far?*

~ *Shut up, brain. Either help me decide what to do here or shut up.*

~ *I'd love to help but you keep changing your mind.*

~ *You're my mind! You stop changing.*

~ *No, I'm your brain. You're your mind. What makes you think your mind's in your brain?*

~ *Can you stop my hands from sweating?*

~ *Ah, involuntary physical reaction while undergoing extreme stress. Sorry, not my department. Blame evolution.*

~ *Brain. Go away.*

~ *Just take it.*

~ *Take what?*

~ *Her hand.*

~ *Just take it?*

~ *There is no right time. Just do it. See what happens.*

Jules looked up at the screen. Then he leant back a little in his chair and peered out of the corner of his eye at Gen. It had taken a lot of hard work to get to this point. Three months they'd been locked up, treated like they'd been caught smoking, stealing and skipping school all at once. Gen had been banished from her attic bedroom and forced to return to sharing with her little sister, Cynthia. Jules had been under a strict regime devised by his dad, Tony, who'd enrolled him in martial arts, piano lessons and extra maths tutoring every night after school so he was never mooching around at home. Tony also had Jules on a strict macrobiotic diet and had forced him to drink wheatgrass juice every morning. Three months of straight home from school and homework checked and early nights. Now finally they'd been allowed a night out but it hadn't been easy to arrange.

His dad had been washing bean shoots and listening to talkback radio discussing public education when Jules had put the question to him. Could he take Gen to the movies on Friday night? Tony had turned around with a frightened look on his face, thrust a handful of wet bean shoots at Jules and then gone immediately to his study to check several books and to ring Jules' mother, Angela.

When Gen had asked her mum, Katherine had leapt up from the couch right in the middle of watching her favourite TV show, which to Gen appeared to be about four old women complaining about not being able to find a boyfriend anywhere on the planet. 'It's starting again. They're planning something,' Katherine had screamed. 'Let me spell this out. En. Oh. Double You. Ay. Why. NO WAY! I have not been through three months of intense therapy and PowerRelaxation to have you two start all this again.'

Gen had raised her eyebrows and backed out of the room, thinking to herself that the therapy and the PowerRelaxation were obviously not enough. Then she went up to the attic room to ask her dad.

After six phone calls back and forth between the two families; after promising to forfeit all future privileges (including phone calls, television and any foods containing sugar or artificial sweeteners or numbered chemical additives); and after a late attempt by Katherine to insist they take Cynthia to see *Lilo and Sitch Three*, permission was finally granted.

That's when Jules' hands had started to sweat.

They sweated as he tried to decide which shirt to wear.

~ *This one? He'd inquired of his brain.*

~ *What? Are you going to a church?*

~ *This is better.*

~ *If you don't want to have any friends.*

~ *Got it. This is perfect.*

~ *Have you smelt that one?*

They sweated as he debated whether to shave.

~ *It's been a week.*

~ *You'll get a rash and you'll slice open that pimple. It'll look worse.*

They sweated as he sat through school on Friday,

information blowing straight through his unfocused head, his brain trying desperately to catch what it could. They sweated as he ate lunch watching Gen huddle with her friends Sonja, Kyeela and Bonnie (who together formed the Four-headed Monster, the four girls who consumed everything around them and spat it back out as gossip and giggles). And as he tried to do his homework as promised, cleaned up as ordered, as he watched the hands on the kitchen clock creep like tired old men round to seven, his palms poured out a slippery treacherous sweat that stained his books and sent dinner plates clattering onto the floor.

And now, here they were still, soggy lumps on the end of his arms about to betray him again.

~ *Thanks, hands.*

~ *I'll pass it on,* promised his brain.

And then in one confident, smooth movement, he moved his right hand across his pants, wiping off the sweat, and slipped it under Gen's, which was resting on the armrest between them. Their fingers interlocked. Gen sat up a little straighter and stared fixedly at the screen.

~ *Excellent! applauded his brain. Well done! Now, can we watch the movie?*

~ *Sure! What's it about?*

FUTURE NOW

TUESDAY MORNING ▶ EARLY FIFTEENTH BILLENNIUM

At the same time, but three thousand years in the future and on a different day, Theodore Pine Four stood to the side of an enormous sound stage.

Next to him fussed Honeydew Meloni. She'd once been Vice Cheeo, Publicity, TimeMaster Corporation – Makers of JumpMan, JumpMan Pro and all the essential TimeJumping Accessories. Then a little glitch at the launch of the new JumpMan Pro three months earlier had been blamed on her. Now she was fourteen-year-old Theo's personal assistant.

Theo was poking about at his hair and gesturing impatiently. Honeydew dived into an unwieldy bag that was weighing down her right shoulder and pulled out a small mirror. Theo tugged at some hair over his forehead, and when he had it arranged to his satisfaction he gave Honeydew a half nod. She dived into the bag again and pulled out a small jar labelled Molecule Follicle Gel.

Unscrewing the lid, Theo scooped a little out then rubbed it through his hair. He focused his concentration until his hair started to change colour. For a moment it was all autumn tones, a dry crackly brown with some very tasteful streaks of russet and a tip or two of gold. Then it went a deep, rich blue, shot through with silver streaks, then swirled like a lollipop before finally turning a bright vibrant lemon all over with just a hint of iridescent white at the tips.

Straightening up, Theo looked inquiringly at Honeydew. She nodded enthusiastically and gave him the two fingers – not pointing up but like a V on its side – which meant yip, Oak Eye, totally boid, you are looking ruly.

Theo agreed with her, particularly after his specially designed HyperCoat subtly adjusted itself to the temperature and the lights, modifying its colour and shape to best contrast with the set and to allow for any developments in fashion that may have occurred since Theo's last public appearance about forty-five minutes earlier. Everyone in Fifteen Billion and Seventy-three had a Coat that could adjust itself to the weather and to fashion. Everyone's Coat was also full of Nanobots and NanoComputers, which could monitor body function and provide complete communications to and from any other Coat on the Two Planets. But no one had a Coat quite as cool as Theo's latest model HyperCoat. It didn't follow fashion – it created fashion.

Theo could barely turn his attention away from himself to concentrate on what was happening out in the centre of the vast auditorium.

Hurrah Banter, the show's host, was getting to the end of her opening spiel. 'The Mayor of Marsville has been having a lot of trouble this week. Been punting a lot of lolla Moonside and now he's scratching his braincase and wondering why his votes are falling like craterfrog upside!'

The crowd *wuhwuhwuhed* with deep appreciation and leant forward together to catch the punchline.

'If he wants the vote to go up, he's gonna have to punt himself Moonside faster than a DustSifter's Snog!'

The crowd exploded. It was a great joke, but like all the greatest jokes, pretty much time specific. You had to be there.

Theo and Honeydew laughed as well. Then Theo took a few deep breaths, because he knew what would be next.

'Anyway, you didn't ClickDown this little show to hear me spattle on. Wherever you are on the Two Planets, the Moon and the asteroids; whenever you might be, whether you're just back from yesterday or you don't know what's happened to tomorrow; and if you're just back from a big Jump – hey it's still Fifteen Billion and Seventy-three, you zip? If you're watching us live or Clicking us Down in the middle of next week, stand by tonight for GrooveBunch – their hit song has been shaking the wax in a lot of ears and everyone says they could be the next big thing for at least twelve hours. We'll also meet the author of *The History of the Cat*, and find out why he thinks they should never be ReGened, but first . .'.

Hurrah paused. She had to. There were thirty thousand people in this room and they all seemed to be screaming.

She held her hands out in a vain attempt to quieten them down. 'I know, I know. I think he's great too ...'

The crowd started stomping on the floor. It was a like a thunderstorm had come indoors.

'Oak Eye, I won't keep you waiting any longer. Here he is, Theodore Pine Four, TimeJumper Numero Uno ...'

Theo breathed in, counted to ten and then walked out from behind the curtain. The *wuhwuhwuhing* and the stomping sounded like an ancient airforce taking off. Thirty thousand people were in rapture at once.

Theo moved towards the centre and then stopped, allowing everyone to see his great-looking Coat, his signature purple shoes and this hour's hair design. He raised a hand, and with a slight nod of the head he managed to convey gratitude and an acknowledgement that he was worth it. He smiled warmly, humbly and assuredly.

His eyes swept the room and he nodded again, waved, and then seemed to pick out someone about seventy rows back. He grinned at them then formed his hands into a little mock pistol and shot them as he winked. He laughed, then moved towards Hurrah Banter, mouthing 'hi' as he shrugged and gestured to the crowd as if to say, what can I do?

Hurrah was a strikingly beautiful woman with cascades of hair that glowed pink and soft mauve and with a cheeky stripe of gold that flashed behind her ears occasionally.

The garment she was wearing appeared to float around her body rather than be attached to it in any way.

She smiled at Theo as though he was her oldest friend in the world and they touched fingertips then brushed cheeks. Theo said something in her ear that made her laugh. She pressed her hand on his arm as she guided him into the chair. Both of them gave the impression that if they weren't here now they'd be having dinner together with other very fabulous and well-dressed people before catching the MarsPod to go ski the Ice Valleys of Olympus Mons.

Eventually everyone quietened down. Then the silence buzzed with expectation.

'Hurrah!'

'Theo – you're looking great. Love the hair. It's really ruly!'

'Thanks, Hurrah. Turn it!'

'Oh, Theo, this?' Hurrah patted her thick luxuriant locks, which would have kept Arctic mammals warm. 'Thank you, but I don't think half the planet's going to be scoping down my look tomorrow.'

This got a big laugh and some warm applause.

'Anyway ...' Hurrah took control of the show. 'Here it is, three months since you escaped from Mil 3, where a gang of TimeHackers using a primitive JumpMan kidnapped you and were threatening to let you fall apart unless you showed them how the new JumpMan Pro really worked. You didn't, and thanks to Quincy Carter One you were rescued. Now you're still the biggest StarLicker in the system. No one has ever lasted three whole months as a celebrity – how are you dealing with it all?'

Theodore Pine was dealing with it like he'd been born to it. It's true that he'd been famous longer than anyone else. Pop bands were considered huge if their song was a hit for three days. Stars of ClickDown shows or writers of ClickBooks – everyone wanted them for a day or two. But three months and everyone still exploding with excitement wherever he went – it had never happened before.

'How am I dealing with it, Hurrah?' Theo looked out at the crowd, who'd gone silent and were staring at him, some with their mouths open, some with their eyes glistening with tears. Four girls in the front row were wearing matching tops, each printed with a single letter, a T, an H, an E, and an O. Except in their excitement they now spelt T, H, O, E. Theo grinned at them and winked, and then turned back to Hurrah, who was leaning forward, a gorgeous, sympathetic smile on her face, her liquid eyes inviting an intimate response.

Theo grinned at her as well. 'Hey, I take it one opening night at a time, you know?' Laughter swelled around him. 'Deal with it, Hurrah? What's to deal with? How do you like the Coat? You know I've got my own line of hair gel now? I'm in the TimeMaster Academy. I think the worst thing I have to deal with is still having to cut my own toenails!'

As Theo expected, applause followed from the laughter. He was discovering that what people wanted from a StarLicker was that they be a StarLicker – it seemed the more he got into it and enjoyed it, the happier everyone was.

Hurrah's smile deepened into one of gratitude. Every time the boy came on, the ClickDown ratings rose 10, 20 per cent. It was amazing.

They chatted on, and then Hurrah wound it up. 'Wip, Theo, I could talk to you all night. But don't you have to go and get ready for something?'

Theo grinned. 'Just a little something.'

'C'mon, what's Quincy launching this time?' Hurrah leaned forward eagerly.

Theo shrugged apologetically. 'Hurrah, even *I* don't know.' And he shrugged again. Hey, this has been a blast, he seemed to be saying. Let's do it again soon!

Hurrah signed off and Theo stood to go.

The audience rose and applauded, as though he'd done something miraculous. Music started up and the screens around the sound stage filled with ads for TimeMaster and HyperCoats and TempoBars.

As Theo walked off Honeydew stepped in and grabbed him by the arm. Hurrah, who'd seemed like his oldest best friend a few minutes ago, ignored him, closing his eyes to let the Cosmetabot do her face again.

Soon Theo was outside the sound stage doors and away from the thousands of adoring fans.

'Quick. There's no way we can be late,' said a slightly worried-looking Honeydew, bustling him into a Pod.

Because even in Theo's daily schedule of fabulous events, the Launch was going to be big. Everyone on the Two Planets, including Theo and Honeydew, wanted to know what Quincy Carter One, Cheeo of TimeMaster Corporation and virtual boss of Earth, had planned this time. Quincy had said, 'Nothing will ever be the same again.' It wasn't a promise you made lightly in a world that can TimeJump.

Jules leant forward. How do you know if a girl wants to kiss you?

> ~ *You don't,* said his brain.
>
> ~ *So what if she doesn't want to kiss me?*
>
> ~ *That you'll know.*

Jules was standing on the porch of Gen's house. Gen's face was about a centimetre and a half away from his.

Everything had gone perfectly. The handholding had been a huge success: Gen's hand had stayed in his for about twenty minutes until, with a gentle smile, she'd finally let go.

After the film they'd walked quietly back to the train station, somehow falling into step in perfect rhythm and with a kind of swaying movement that meant they knocked against each other a lot. They'd talked about the last three months, how over the top their parents had been, how bizarre the whole thing was, how it was all starting to seem like some kind of dream. Were they really visited by Theodore Pine Four? Had Gen really gone to watch a Pyramid being built? Had Jules been to the future and then back to the Big Bang itself? They laughed at the way they were now really interested in history and were reading lots of books. Jules had started to tell Gen the story about how some archaeologists digging through the ruins of ancient Pompeii had discovered a pair of modern trainers under a bed and Gen had finished it off. She'd read it in the paper as well. There was great debate as to whether it was a prank and how anyone could have put a pair of shoes in a room that hadn't seen the light of day for two thousand years. Jules had wished they could just keep on walking and talking like this forever.

But they'd had to catch the train and get back home.

And now here they were, standing together on Gen's front porch with five minutes to spare, and it was time to say goodnight.

~ *She's not moving,* Jules said to his brain.

~ *That's good.*

~ *I'm going to do it all wrong.*

~ *Probably. But look, I'm your brain, right? I've watched you learn a lot of things. I remember trying to get your chubby little fingers to pick up blocks. And then toilet training —*

~ *Yeah, OK, can we go over this some other time? I think it's about to happen.*

Jules had a moment of panic, worse than he'd felt when he'd been lost in the future or when he was being chased by Neanderthals in the past.

~ What do I do? Does she know what to do?

~ Maybe. You'll need to tilt your head to one side.

~ What?

~ The nose. You have to make some room for the nose.

~ Which side? Left?

~ Sure. Tilt your head to the left.

~ No, right. I'm going to go right.

~ OK. Right.

~ I'm not sure.

~ DO IT NOW!

Jules went left. Gen turned her head a little to her left as well. He was staring into her eye. Gen smiled at him, looked down, back into his eyes and then just moved her head forward a little, closing her eyes as she did.

Jules could feel the heat of her face, and a soft, warm smell wafted up his nostrils that made him feel lightheaded and powerful all at once.

Opening his mouth and licking his lips – he screamed.

Gen leapt back, like he'd bitten her on the nose. Then she screamed as well.

Standing next to them was a thin, bony man with a long, weathered face. His eyes were intense and they flicked back and forth from Gen to Jules like a lizard choosing which fly to eat for breakfast. His clothes looked like he'd been wearing them for weeks. And he was standing just a little too close for comfort.

'Sorry,' he said, scratching a bit and looking nervously about. 'This is not a good time. I'll go away and come back earlier.'

'You! I know you.' Gen was still screaming. Then her voice dropped to a hiss. 'You're that guy. Franklin!'

Franklin? thought Jules. Who's Franklin? How did he just appear like that? And why, instead of experiencing my first real live kiss with a real live girl, am I being interrupted by him? And why does Gen know who he is? And why does he smell bad? And why —

But Jules stopped asking himself questions because the strange, skinny, smelly guy was asking him one. 'Who are you? Go home. I need to talk to her.'

'Can you keep your voice down?' ordered Gen. 'What are you doing here, Franklin? And why do you TimeJumpers always appear so suddenly?'

'How else are we going to appear?' shrugged Franklin. 'Bit hard to make an appointment from three thousand years in the future.'

'You're a TimeJumper!' said Jules. 'From Fifteen Billion and Seventy-three?'

Franklin grabbed him by the arm and put his face up close to his. 'Who are you? How do you know so much!'

'Owww!' Franklin's long bony fingers and nails were digging into Jules' arm. 'I'm, I'm Jules. I've Jumped. Who are you? Are you a friend of Theo's?'

At the mention of Theo's name, Franklin dropped Jules' arm and cast more nervous glances about. He scuttled out into the darkness and then back into the pool of light on the porch.

Staring at them he muttered and tapped his teeth. Then he beckoned them into a huddle, and casting another glance over his shoulder, he said, 'Know where I can get a little TimeHacking action? Hip me to it, huh? Maybe you know someone who knows someone?' This was accompanied by lots of winks and nods and fingers on the side of the nose.

Jules hadn't heard of TimeHacking. But he had heard of TimeJumping, and last time he'd done it there'd been a JumpMan, a hovering silver sphere with a red remote. Franklin didn't seem to have one.

'Where's your JumpMan?' Jules asked.

'JumpMan?' Franklin all but spat. 'What, you think I'd use one of Quincy's little toys?' And he pulled back a filthy sleeve to reveal a sleek panel as thick as a biscuit and moulded to his arm.

Jules looked at Franklin's device in amazement. Like Theo's JumpMan, it didn't have much on it – just a screen and a couple of buttons. But somehow in there was enough computing power to send a person or two anywhere and anywhen there was a decent JumpSite. From the Big Bang till yesterday. Fifteen billion years of history to explore. No wonder JumpMans were popular. From where Franklin and Theo had come, three thousand years in the future, a future where they calculated the date from the beginning of time, every kid had one. Come the weekend, no one was home – they were all having a fantastic time watching a Maori War Party go into action, or Marching with Napoleon to Moscow or – for the more refined – watching Mozart Compose or perhaps enjoying a Day with Da Vinci. And they all did it with TimeMaster JumpMans.

Jules took a closer look. On the screen of Franklin's JumpMan he could read Gen's address and the date. It seemed like Franklin had meant to come here.

'This is a JumpMan, my friend, if you must use that term,' Franklin said with a sneer. I wanted to call them a Temporal Tempter but, as usual, Quincy got his way. Oh no, this', and Franklin tapped the device on his arm, 'is not one of those pathetic, overwired coconuts Quincy has turned into a fashion accessory and flogged off to the kids. This uses my own Franklin Nixon ChronoMatic Lock Sequencer, Pre- and Post-Particle Oscillating Search Transfer System, and it calculates not just the distance from the Big Bang but also the distance from the next Universe Renewal Cycle, giving you WhenLock Accuracy that is beyond anything copycat Quincy has ever come up with. The Quantum Computers in this little wizz —'

'Franklin,' Gen interrupted. 'That's fascinating, but the last time I saw you, you were trying to grab one of those overwired coconuts off Theo and me! Which would have left us stranded forever at the Great Pyramid. And then you just disappeared. What are you doing here? What do you want? And can you keep it down a bit? Do you want everyone to hear you?'

Franklin shrugged. 'Oh, yip, yip, sorry about that. I was a bit desperate. There's only so much sand and sun worship you can stand. You want to know what happened? Quincy Carter One's what happened. He Jumped me out. Now he wants to get rid of me again. But let's get down to it. I need to move a little Time about. Hack it. Sack it. Piggyback it. Know what I'm saying?'

Jules and Gen had no idea what he was saying. They both just wanted him to say it a little more quietly.

Then Franklin bent forward and peered into their faces. 'So what happened to *you*?' he demanded.

Gen stepped back. 'Franklin! What is going on? I've got no idea what you're talking about. What are you doing here? You don't make any sense and I want you to leave. You're going to get us into trouble! Go on, just JumpOff or Back or Hack or whatever you do. I don't know that I want anything to do with TimeJumping again. All it's done so far is ruin my life.'

Good on you Gen, thought Jules. Let's get rid of him.

Wasn't this the same as last time? As soon as he got close to Gen, bang! Someone from Fifteen Billion and Seventy-three dropped by to ruin everything. Couldn't Franklin come back tomorrow? Or not at all?

'All right, all right.' Franklin backed off a little. 'Just take a quick peeky boo at this, Oak Eye?'

Franklin smoothed an area on the front of his Coat. Franklin's Coat was so ragged and filthy, Jules hadn't realised it was a Coat like the one Theo had worn. Now Franklin rubbed some dirt off the front panel and a screen appeared accompanied by a soft fanfare. Jules was impressed. The quality of the graphics and sound was very good.

'Welcome to HyperCoat AV Presentations,' Franklin's Coat said in a full, creamy voice. 'Please select from the following options. To view anything experienced in the last three hours please say "Three Hours" —'

'Yip, zip it Coat,' barked Franklin. 'The Theo stuff, just play the Theo stuff.'

'I'm sorry,' replied the Coat. 'Did you say the Leo stuff? For Astrology, just say your star sign —'

'Aaaargggh! It was easier with papyrus and bits of sharp metal! These Coats! They do everything except what you want them to do! Theo, Theo, Theo, get me the Theo grabs I clicked into five minutes ago, you useless piece of rag.'

Jules wished Franklin would hurry up. But still, here was someone from the future who had a Coat with video. It was worth a look. He just didn't want to get caught, because this time, they wouldn't be grounded. This time, they'd be sent to boarding schools far away, run by obscure religious orders who believed in cold showers and regular beatings as a way of keeping young people in check.

'Umm, Gen,' Jules ventured, thinking to suggest that Franklin might come back at a more convenient time.

But Gen wasn't listening. She was watching Theo on the *Hurrah Banter Show* on the screen on Franklin's Coat. Jules took a closer look. There was the back of Theo's gorgeous designer HyperCoat, complete with a huge handstitched TimeMaster logo. There were thousands of people and you could sense the enormous excitement Theo generated as he walked into the room. Jules was amazed at how confident and experienced Theo appeared. He did all the things talk show guests always do and seemed to be doing it very naturally, like he'd been doing it forever. His hair looked amazing and he was chatting with the host like they were old friends. Jules leant forward a little to hear what they were saying.

Hurrah was talking. '. . . three months since you escaped from Mil 3, where a gang of TimeHackers using a primitive JumpMan kidnapped you and were threatening to let you fall apart unless you showed them how the new JumpMan Pro really worked. You didn't, and thanks to Quincy Carter One you were rescued . . .'

'What did she just say?' blurted Gen.

'She said you were a ruthless gang of TimeHackers,' said Franklin.

'We didn't kidnap him!' said Gen indignantly. 'He just turned up in my bedroom and then he couldn't go home.'

'I knew you weren't TimeHackers,' said Franklin. 'Why does everyone believe that story? Look where we are – it's Mil 3. Giddy clones, is that a light bulb?' Franklin squinted up at the light over the porch. 'Zip, you probably *know* Edison, right? Zif you're going to be TimeHacking. You don't even know what Time is. Nip, worse, you don't even know what *time* it is!'

He snorted. 'It's Mil 3,' he yelled. 'Go inside the house. There'll be little clocks blinking everywhere and they'll all have different times on them!'

How does he know that, thought Jules, thinking of the clocks in his own kitchen. The one on the oven hadn't moved at all since it became a home for cockroaches, the one in the microwave was set on summer time, and the one in the radio was seven minutes slow. His watch was usually kind of close . . .

'Zif they could have kidnapped Theo!' Franklin was chuckling and dancing about a little.

Gen was still watching Theo on the screen. 'Are they making out he's some kind of hero or something?' She looked up at Franklin. 'What's going on? Is Theo all right?'

'Huh, is Theo all right?' repeated Franklin. 'He's more popular than breathing. The entire Two Planets have gone pineapple about him. He's on everything, he's selling everything, they've got ads on the back of Pods for TheoBars – you can't ClickDown a BulSheet that doesn't have a story on him. Never seen anything like it. He's Lindbergh.'

'He's what?' asked Jules.

'Lindbergh – first solo flight across the Atlantic. You gotta Jump on Lindy one day. It's great. He flies this little plane out of St Louis in America, all on his own. You can sit right there with him. He's so calm. He's a nobody. And then when he touches down in Paris – the world goes double pineapple. Everyone wants a piece of him. You've never heard of him?'

Both Jules and Gen shook their head.

'Huh. And I thought we'd lost history in Billenium Fifteen. At least we've got the excuse that we were stuck on Mars for three millennia. You guys, you throw history away like it happened yesterday. Like it doesn't matter.'

Jules was reminded of what Theo had told them about his Now, the world of Fifteen Billion and Seventy-three. Everyone lived on Mars after being evacuated from Earth.

And they'd only just started to come back to Earth to repopulate it. TimeJumping had been developed to help people rediscover the history of the planet that humans hadn't lived on for three thousand years. Instead it had turned into the biggest leisure activity for kids anyone had ever seen.

Franklin shook his head sadly. 'Anyway, Theo is famous. He's the biggest StarLicker we've ever seen.'

'StarLicker?'

'Yip, StarLicker. You know, famous, a celebrity. They rise so high they can lick the stars. Wanna see some more?'

Jules started to say no, not that it hadn't been great to catch up with what Theo was doing but it was getting late and maybe he really should be thinking about going home.

But Gen said, louder, 'Yeah, what else have you got? How come he's lying about it all, too? Does he ever mention us at all?'

Franklin had been scrolling through recordings as she spoke. 'Nip, ooh, except for this.'

Franklin ordered the Coat to show them more of Theo, and after the Coat turned itself into a snowsuit, showed them a clip of the Duke Ellington Orchestra and measured Franklin's cholesterol and blood pressure, which actually rose while it was being taken, it finally did.

There was a close up shot of Theo. He looked moody and kind of handsome. His hair was sepia blue, and he was answering questions in an extremely serious way. The close-up widened and revealed that he was sitting up the front of a lecture hall full of students. They were slouched down in their chairs as students do, and they were doing their best to look as though they didn't care, but they were all listening with rapt attention.

'So, you know,' Theo was saying, 'it's great to be here at the TimeMaster Academy for Advanced SiteSearching, and I mean I can't tell you guys anything about Entry/Exit Sequence, or RLA Techniques but I can I just say this.' Theo looked around the hall, pausing like a professional and adopting a deep and sincere look on his face. 'You've gotta believe in yourself.'

Theo was now nodding as if he'd just imparted something very personal and very real to the students. The footage was beautifully edited, cutting between close-ups of his hands, his fingers running through his hair, and attentive, gorgeous-looking students, and moody close-ups of Theo's face.

Jules' heart sank. He'd always felt like something had happened between Gen and Theo. Now, seeing her watch this clip, he wondered how he could compete with someone so well produced.

'When you're out there, and local time is running down,' Theo was saying, as some gentle yet inspirational music began in the background, 'it's just you and the universe.

If you don't believe in yourself, you know, you're not going to find a way back home.'

'Oh please, Franklin, what's happened to him?' asked Gen, a pained expression on her face. 'He was a big enough tosser when he got here, but at least by the time he left he was nearly normal. No, don't tell me. He's just about to tell them, "Hey it is true, you can live your dreams".'

'. . . live your dreams,' echoed Theo on the screen.

Gen made a retching, groaning sound.

Jules grinned happily.

'Zip!' said Franklin. 'I want you to hear this.'

A girl with fluoro-lime hair stood up to ask a question. 'Even though you were, like, kidnapped and that,' she said, 'did you form any kind of relationship with them? I mean the TimeHackers? Could you talk to them and that?'

Theo swallowed and looked down. The room had gone very still and silent.

'There was a girl. She looked after me. I don't know that I'll ever see her again. Mil 3's a pretty hostile world, but I felt like we connected.'

'What was her name?' the green-haired girl asked.

'Genevieve. Genevieve Corrigan,' Theo replied quietly.

Franklin stopped the recording. Gen stood very still and Jules suddenly felt an overwhelming interest in the camelias by the front door.

'So the worst thing that happened to him with the evil TimeHackers here in Mil 3 was he got a crush on you!' Franklin poked a grimy finger at Gen. Then he shook his head ruefully. 'There's something very wrong with this. It stinks like rotting valar juice, which doesn't stink that good when it's fresh. You can't just Jump somewhere visible by mistake. None of this was an accident. Maybe it wasn't meant to be Theo but someone was thinking of coming here.'

He slapped his hands together. 'Rip! That settles it. I've had a brilliant idea. You're coming back with me!'

'Wh-what?' said Jules, looking up from the camelias.

'Lip, let's go! Let's Jump,' said Franklin, grabbing them. 'You can really help me. Quincy is planning something. I don't know what. But Quincy does not do anything for fun. He was never fun, he doesn't know how to have fun. If Quincy had your co-ordinates programmed into the JumpMan Theo used to get here, then all of this has something to do with you. So come on, let's go! Back in my Now Quincy and Theo are about to make some huge announcement. The entire population's gone triple pineapple. You can take a peek and see what they're up to.' He did the lizard thing with his eyes again. 'So you want to help, or you just want to smooch on here for a while?'

Jules would have been pretty happy to smooch on,

really. In fact, he'd been hoping to get that started when Franklin turned up. But the thought of going back to Theo's Time again was exciting. He didn't really know what Franklin was talking about, but how could he say no to another chance to TimeJump?

Gen was feeling even more conflicted. She'd loved TimeJumping the last time, too. But what was Theo going on about? And why did boys either ignore you or go all weird on you? It was so confronting and confusing. And why did Franklin want them to go, anyway? What was he talking about? Was there any reason to trust this strange smelly man who licked his lips and tapped his teeth?

And then, just as Franklin was ordering his JumpMan to respond to Voice command, the front door of the house was flung open.

Until this very moment, Gen's mother, Katherine Corrigan, was well on the way to recovery. Counselling three times a week had almost convinced her that she could trust herself again. The constant feeling of doubt that nothing was real and that somehow at any moment she would start seeing figures in the room, or see herself on the other side of the room, or see people suddenly disappear – that feeling was starting to fade. Her therapist was very happy with her progress and suggested that, in a matter of weeks, she would stop believing her daughter might disappear at any moment or that she was keeping aliens with strange hair and even stranger powers in her room. Her therapist had almost convinced her that when Gen said nothing had been going on she'd been telling the truth, and had helped her realise that her own beliefs could not be real because they were simply impossible. She'd felt terrific while Gen had been out and was only just saying so to Gen's father in the lounge room. 'See?' she'd said. 'I can trust her to go out. I'm not worried. She'll come home and everything will be back to normal.'

But then, over the noise of the television, she thought she heard a scream and then other strange sounds. Finally she'd got up, walked to the front door, opened it, and was now standing there looking at her daughter and her friend, Jules, and a skinny, dirty man who was hanging onto their arms.

The skinny man's Coat started to speak. 'Now hear this. Now hear this,' broadcast the Coat. 'This is a Third Party Detection Alarm. TimePresent intruder. Abort mission, Activate TimeSweep last thirty seconds.'

Katherine felt dizzy, like someone in an old movie falling into a spiral. Her brain rejected what she was seeing and hearing.

The man released Jules for one second, slap a strange-looking device on his arm, and heard him cackle and yell, 'No time like the present!' And everyone on her front porch disappeared.

Katherine stood, mouth open, swaying slightly as she found herself suddenly alone.

And then she felt good. She hadn't gone mad! The therapist was wrong. Her daughter had been lying to her. She was involved in something bizarre that meant people appeared and disappeared. She was right to be haunted by this feeling and to be constantly checking that things were solid and real, because as she had just seen they could disappear at any moment! She couldn't even trust her memory because she knew that soon she would start to forget this moment, but never completely. There would always be a faint sense of it. She would remember it as you might remember a show you saw as a very young child – just the mood, perhaps one scene. Enough to convince you that it had happened, but not enough to convince others.

Katherine turned and went back inside. She felt truly wonderful, and started to skip and sing a little. Then she stopped. Maybe she didn't exist! Maybe *she* isn't really here. What is *here* anyway? Maybe we're not really *here*, we just perceive ourselves as *here* and how do we know that what *we* perceive is in any way accurate? Maybe she only imagines that Genevieve is her daughter? Maybe reality is that she's *not*. When she disappears, perhaps that's reality. Oh these were exciting and wonderful thoughts. If only she could share them! Unsure where her next footstep would take her Katherine went into what might or might not be her front room.

Her husband, Steven, looked at her and said, 'Oh no, Katie. Come on, it's not happening again, is it?'

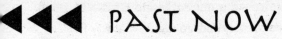
Lavinia sighed to herself. Latin. Why did she have to sit here learning Latin? Her tutor, Claudius, was short and scratched himself too much. It was hot, and even the dust hanging in the sunlight seemed listless. There was a tiny window high above her, and she wished she could jump up and slip out through it. It wasn't going to happen. She would be here for at least another hour. Stuck on a hard chair, in a stuffy room with Claudius, his thin, piping, annoying voice droning on and on and on.

Virgil.

Some poet who didn't know when to shut up. Endless lines about Rome and its glory. The tiresome journeys of some hero called Aeneas who always won out in the end. It was so boring. Why couldn't it be more exciting? If she and her brothers had to sit here learning Latin, couldn't it be stories about princesses and the princes who fell in love with them? Or stories of the Gods – they were always good. Down they'd come from the mountain top, change themselves into a horse and start arguing with the sea. Pow! There'd be a clash of thunder and someone would be locked into a rock for an age until Zeus himself sat down for a rest on the boulder one afternoon and heard the tiny voice of the imprisoned immortal inside. Crack! The God was free and then off they'd all go again. That was fun.

Or tell some jokes – if there were any jokes in Latin. Didn't seem to be when Claudius was teaching it. The last time they'd laughed during Latin was about a month after Claudius came. Her brothers had released a scorpion in the classroom. It had scuttled up to the front and Claudius had leapt on the table, screaming like a girl. They'd laughed until their father beat them and sent them to their rooms for the night with no food. Every now and again one of her brothers would catch her eye and make a little scuttling gesture with his fingers in the direction of their fearful teacher and they would smile as they shared the memory. But even that didn't happen very often any more.

Lavinia looked around at her four brothers. They hadn't heard a word Claudius had said in three years. They spent the entire time devising plots to fool their father into letting them ride out into the forest. Or planning to run away and join the army. Or just asleep. Her youngest brother claimed he could stare straight at Claudius with his eyes open, even though he was actually sound asleep. Claudius had long ago stopped asking them questions. Now he tended to both ask and answer questions himself. If he'd waited for any of them to answer, they'd just sit there all day. He may as well ask the dust, swirling slowly through the beams of light. Or perhaps he didn't ask them anything, any more, because he knew they couldn't answer, and then he would have to admit that he'd taught them nothing and that the finer points of language were lost on them. In fact, it was not only the finer points of Latin that were lost on them but all of the rough and quite plain points as well. And so he plodded on through Virgil, stopping every three words or so to ask himself a little question about a detail of how this language worked.

This has to agree with that. These are plural. That's subjunctive, if indeed it were subjunctive. Lavinia couldn't remember and couldn't care less. Why sit here learning Latin? It was, after all, the language she spoke every day.

ZONE ▶ TIMEKEEPER'S GREENWICH, EARTH
ITEM ▶ 994753C-211-6348220/TIM082
VIEW ▶ Current time at the All-Time Clock

YEAR 15,000,000,073   MONTHS 9   DAYS 27   HOURS 14.30   SECONDS 28
NANOSECONDS 45378206637   ARCOSECONDS 261885927483

1,5,000,000,073 9 27 14.30 28 45378206637 261885927483

chapter two

It's About Time

 **FUTURE NOW**
TUESDAY LUNCHTIME ▶ EARLY FIFTEENTH BILLENNIUM

Jules opened his eyes. He'd been TimeJumped. Was it something you could get used to? The sudden transference of your entire self and your trainers to not just somewhere else, but somewhen else?

Even though he'd done it before, Jules still had the same reaction he'd had the very first time. It just can't be possible.

You can't go back and forward through time, like you're finding a spot on some cosmic DVD. You just can't.

Time goes forward. Time is something that goes along, minute after minute, unrolling itself out like an infinite tape measure. You can't roll the tape measure up, or run back to the start of it, or scurry up ahead. Can you?

One second ticks off after the other at the rate of one second at a time.

Don't they?

And they've been doing that from when time began and will continue to do that until time ends. Won't they?

And you, yourself, you are in your allotted slice of time. You've got about eight billion seconds and they're yours. They start when you start, they tick away as you tick away and they stop when you stop. You can't just bang a computer and whip yourself off into some other Time.

It just can't be possible.

~ *Forget about it,* said his brain.

~ *You forget about it,* replied Jules.

~ *Yes, well actually I can. I put these questions into the memory files. It's you that keep on getting them out. And would you mind putting them back again when you've finished?*

~ *But it can't be possible.*

~ *Well, where are you now then? Round at your friend Max's place?*

Jules had to admit that he wasn't round at his friend Max's place. For one thing, Max didn't live in a cave. Jules looked around. Not a particularly pleasant cave, either. It was more the sort of cave mushrooms and pale slugs might enjoy.

How he'd got here Jules still didn't understand. He knew you couldn't TimeJump to school every day. He knew that usually you could only Jump to places where there was a JumpSite, but how TimeJumping actually worked, Jules had no idea.

Not that Jules was alone in having no understanding of how TimeJumping worked. Even in the fifteenth billennium it was a question people didn't really worry much about. People asked, of course. They'd take their new JumpMan out of the box, admire the gorgeous metallic sphere, a little smaller than a basketball, a little bigger than a grapefruit, pick up the red remote and poke at a few buttons, and then they'd invariably set it to hovering in front of them and say, How can this thing possibly contain enough computing power to track every particle in the human body, shift them ten nanoseconds out of the present and then relocate and reassemble those same particles in an exact JumpSite somewhere and somewhen in the last fifteen billion years of history?

The question was right, the answer was, to most people, incomprehensible. Theo had told them that it was really only the original TimeMaster Six, the team that discovered the techniques of TimeJumping back in the late fourteenth billennium, and a few of their close friends who listened very hard whenever it was explained to them, who had any idea of what was involved in moving a human body from one Time to another.

Really, there was no way you could possibly understand unless you were born a genius. And not just really smart, but once-in-a-century Einstein kind of genius. You had to be the kind of kid who was studying physics and playing simultaneous chess on three continents by the time you're about three and a half – if you were that kind of kid, then you might get your head around it.

But as most people at three and a half are usually still blobbing about and dribbling on themselves, and thinking they're pretty clever because they haven't put the square peg in the round hole, you can see why they will never understand how you can build computers the size of a speck of dust that are powerful enough to do all the calculations necessary to Jump someone somewhere and somewhen else.

No wonder everyone just stopped asking and thinking about it and concentrated on what a JumpMan could do.

A JumpMan could take you anywhen you liked, from the Big Bang till Yesterday, as TimeMaster liked to print on its buttonless shirts. You want to have breakfast with an Atzec Prince? Fine, hope you like cocoa on your iguana. You want to see the Beatles performing at the Cavern in Liverpool?

Fine, hope you like the sound of screaming girls, because you won't be hearing that much of John Lennon singing. You want to be plucked from your front porch by a bony madman and hurled three thousand years into the future to the year Fifteen Billion and Seventy-three? Probably not, so it's understandable that when it happened to Jules and Gen they were not only amazed and intrigued by the miraculous process of TimeJumping. They were a little upset that it had happened at all.

'Franklin! What have you done?' Gen was sitting right beside Jules and her shouting brought him firmly into the present he was now in. There was something dripping down Jules' neck, and the rocks under his hand felt slimy. He took a closer look at his surroundings. They were sitting in darkness, but up one end of the cave where there was a little more light Jules could see a long metallic workbench covered in wires, bits of metal and plastic, tools and a host of other stuff he didn't recognise. Stuck to the wall, like posters in a bedroom, were several flat cloth screens. Watching the screens intently was Franklin.

'Franklin! Answer me!' Gen tried again. 'This is kidnapping! You are holding us against our will. It's illegal. It's against all notions of human rights. I'll complain to the United Nations.' Gen had a strong sense of justice, and not only when something unjust happened to her. She'd decided she didn't trust Franklin one bit. Most of all, she hated other people making decisions for her. Wasn't she virtually fourteen? Wasn't she old enough to have a say?

Franklin barely glanced at them. He was focused on the monitors.

'Frankleeeeeeeen!' Gen had stood up and was now beating her fists on Franklin's back. 'Don't ignore me! I want to go back. Now!'

Franklin whirled around. 'What? What is your problem?' Franklin seemed astonished by Gen's reaction.

'The problem? You just up and Jumped us. You could have asked. And in front of my mother! Do you know how bad the last three months have been? Do you know how long it's taken our parents to calm down after last time? They're going to kill us. We're not just going to be grounded. We're going to be buried, and never allowed out. That's the problem, Franklin.'

Franklin shrugged. 'I'll Jump you back before you left.'

'What?' snapped Gen.

'I'll Jump you back to just before I turned up. It'll be like you never left. Your mother will never know.'

'But she saw us go this time. She'll remember that.'

'I left a TimeSweep going. It adjusts events, clears her memory. She won't recall it. You'll Jump back to a couple of minutes ago, smooch your boyfriend, your mother will open the door and there you go. In the meantime, you might be useful here, Oak Eye?'

'Oh, it's not going to work like that,' moaned Gen. 'Why do you lot always pretend it's going to be so smooth. I mean, Theo's Jump last time was a huge stuff-up, wasn't it? None of your Rewinds and TimeSweeps and Code Cop clean-ups helped then.'

'Look! There's Theo,' Jules said. He was too excited about being back in the future to get as worked up as Gen. He jumped up and pointed at the screens. On one there was an outdoor stage set up and a huge crowd gathering. On the other was Theo.

Gen moved a little closer. 'When are we?' she asked.

'It's my Now, when else?' said Franklin. 'Fifteen Billion and Seventy-three. You got Pods like that in your Now?'

On the screen was a small transport Pod zipping along a thin rail. Sitting inside it was Theo and a woman.

'Where's he going?' asked Gen.

'To Quincy's big parade! His "Launch",' replied Franklin. 'And you're going too.'

'I'm sorry?' said Jules.

'You're going too. That was my brilliant idea. Quincy's after me, so I can't go in and find out what's going on. But you can.'

Jules and Gen stared at one another and then at Franklin, who was looking at them like he'd asked them to go to the shops to get some milk.

'You want us to *spy* on Theo?'

'Oh, it's slow with you Mil 3 people, isn't it? Remind me, is it you lot who landed on the Moon and then never went back?'

Gen folded her arms, curled her upper lip to its most extreme, and gave Franklin a scathing look that Jules recognised from school. It was the one she and the other members of the Four-headed Monster gave those they regarded as total dweeb nerdie dorks.

But it didn't work on Franklin. In fact, Jules noticed that Franklin didn't really seem to be looking at them. He was looking in their direction, but not really ever making eye contact.

Franklin leaned back on the bench. 'Look. Here's the situation.' He paused and looked up at the ceiling for a while. 'Theo dropped into your bedroom, right?'

Gen nodded.

'Why? Why did he turn up at your place? Why you?'

Gen shrugged. 'It was just a mistake, an accident.'

'Quincy doesn't make mistakes. Well, he made a mistake that night, but it wasn't the place that was mistaken. It was the person. *Theo* wasn't meant to go there but someone else was. Someone who's interested in you.'

Gen frowned. She shivered a little and wondered whether to believe Franklin or not. He twitched and fiddled with everything. He hopped about and tapped his teeth.

'Why should we trust you?' she asked quietly. 'It's just you telling us this stuff. Maybe you're the bad guy? Maybe you're trying to hurt Theo. Maybe Quincy's the good guy and you're trying to bring him down. How would we know?'

~ *You never think of stuff like this, do you?*

~ *I'm sorry, brain?* said Jules. *What about you? You ever think of stuff like this?*

~ *All the time. You just choose to ignore it.*

~ *Do I?*

~ *Believe me. I'm your brain. I think of everything. What you choose to think about is up to you.*

~ *I'll have to think about that.*

~ *Good choice.*

Franklin sat back on his stool and looked in Gen's direction with a certain grudging respect. 'Hmmph,' he snorted. 'Take a look at Theo.' He pointed at one of his screens. 'You know he's getting out of the Pod with his personal assistant? I mean, what fourteen-year-old needs a personal assistant? He's not famous because of what happened with you guys. He's famous because Quincy wants him to be famous. Quincy needs him to be famous. But why? Wip, what have you got to lose? You're here now. Go and see Theo. If you still don't believe there's something funny going on, I'll Jump you back, it'll be like it never happened. Soneehaha, see you when the Universe ends. Oh, and by the way, you're invisible.'

Jules looked down at himself. He was invisible? He could still see his second-best jeans and his coolest shirt, which he'd put on to go to the movies with Gen only hours before.

He could see his hands; if he touched his arm he still felt *all there.* Then he looked at Gen.

'You can see yourselves and each other,' said Franklin, as if he was reading their thoughts. 'You've been TimeJumped in so you're both ten nanoseconds behind local time, hence invisible. But I can't see you, and look, no reflection.' He held up a sheet of shiny metal.

Jules moved to where he would normally be able to see himself but all that was reflected was the cave wall behind him. He wasn't there.

Gen came over and stood next to him. Her mouth fell open and she reached out to touch the reflective metal as though there must be something wrong with it.

'But we saw you? You were visible,' said Jules.

'Oh yip, you *can* Jump visible. That's no big trick. I *needed* you to see me. But just because you can doesn't mean you should.'

Franklin rested the sheet of metal on the bench and turned to show them his reflection. 'In fact, I think that might be the problem.'

He picked at his teeth in the mirror and then wiped his fingers on his Coat.

'Sip. You wanna help?' He looked left and right. 'Are you two nodding, or what?'

Back in Mil 3, the hour was ticking by. Time hadn't stopped for those who hadn't Jumped. At Gen's place Cynthia was alternating between looking out the window at the front porch, in case Jules and Gen reappeared or anyone else turned up, and running back to listen at the top of the stairs as her father tried to find out from her mother what had happened.

But Cynthia knew what had happened. She had seen it all. She'd been waiting up for Gen to come home. She knew that if there was going to be any trouble, it would happen then, and she couldn't bear to miss it.

If she pressed her face against her bedroom window she could just see the front porch. She'd been a bit disappointed when Jules and Gen had come home ten minutes early, then elated when they looked like they were going to kiss. She could hold that over Gen for months. And then she'd been so excited she could barely sit still when the skinny man had turned up. She knew what was going on. She remembered Theo. She'd seen him. No one had believed her then but she wouldn't make any mistakes this time.

She raced back to the top of the stairs.

In the lounge room, Steven was asking Katherine as calmly as he could to tell him what had happened.

Katherine was singing, making up lyrics to a tune from a film she'd loved as a child.

'*Chim Chiminey, Chim Chiminey, Chim Chim Cher-oop!*

'*My children can fly to the sky, up they swoop!*'

Cynthia hugged herself. This was going to be great!

The phone rang.

Steven got up and answered it. 'Tony, mate,' he said. 'No, no, not here.'

There was a pause while he listened to Jules' dad. 'Well, I'm kind of stuck here, really. Cynthia's in bed and Katherine —' Steven paused as Katherine waltzed past him, now singing nursery rhymes.

'*Hey diddle diddle, the cat and the fiddle*

'*My Gen jumps over the moon.*

'*That Jules boy laughs to see such fun*

'*And they both ran away with the spoon!*'

Steven picked up the conversation.

'Ahh, Katherine's gone a bit – you know – so I don't really want to go out. Could you? You gonna drive into town to see if you can see them? Good on ya, mate.'

Steven hung up the phone and went out into the kitchen to see what his wife was up to. Cynthia decided to return to her spot at the window. Her mother being a bit batty and her father trying to deal with it was old news.

Cynthia wanted to be there when Gen and Jules turned up again. Halfway there she had an idea. Video! Why just watch? Why not record them turning up again?

She snuck into her parents' bedroom, found the video camera and then headed back to her room. She grinned her wicked little grin. Brilliant! She'd get them this time.

At Jules' place, Tony Santorini looked around for his car keys. He felt sick with worry and disappointment. Why hadn't Jules come straight home? What had happened? What had he done wrong? Was it diet? Was he being too strict, was he not being strict enough?

There was a knock on the door.

Thank God, he thought, and sprinted to the door and flung it open. It wasn't Jules. It was a pizza delivery boy.

'Carter?' the boy said. 'One large Supreme, extra garlic?'

Tony shook his head, assured the boy that he wasn't called Carter and that he hadn't ordered a pizza.

When the boy had gone Tony went out to his car. He drove off into the night without any real idea where to look for them.

►►► FUTURE NOW

TUESDAY LUNCHTIME ► EARLY FIFTEENTH BILLENNIUM

'Door!' ordered Franklin.

The door slid open and they stepped through.

They were in a back alley in a city.

'Door close!' ordered Franklin, and the door slid shut. Now it looked like any rocky outcrop you might find in a back alley in any city in Fifteen Billion and Seventy-three.

Jules stopped and looked back at the door. 'Where are we?' he asked.

'Shhh!' hissed Franklin. 'Don't forget. You're invisible, but people can still hear you.'

Jules couldn't see anyone anywhere. 'While there's nobody about, could you please tell us where we are?'

'This', said Franklin, as they came around a corner and into a main square, 'is Metro One. The only city on Earth. When I last saw it, forty years ago, it had so much promise. Now, it's crowded, messy and everything we planned it wouldn't be. Disgusting!'

Neither Jules nor Gen could see anything disgusting about Metro One. Compared with their own city, this one was spacious, busy but not crowded. In fact, nothing matched their ideas of what a city should be.

Cities are meant to be all squares and grids. Roads runs

in straight lines; alongside them run kerbs. There might be strips of grass, a sapling or two in a cage, a footpath and a wall. If there is some greenery, it will be in a park, itself a neat square divided off from everything else. In Mil 3, buildings were built beside the roads – they marched down streets next door to one another, and rose in straight lines towards the sky. Each floor would, in the main, be the same distance above the one below it.

None of that applied to Metro One. Not even a little bit.

Metro One wasn't built over the landscape. It kind of grew out of it. At what would normally be street level there was just bush and grass, and rocks and trees. There were no roads – the only transport through this square were the thin silver rails the Pods ran on. Buildings seemed to be supported by very little, appearing to start many metres above the ground. Or in some cases the earth and the trees sort of flowed in the front door. Not that many of the buildings seemed to have a front door. But sometimes there was *only* a door, suggesting that the rest of the building was underneath the ground.

Whole hillsides slid open to reveal foyers and lobbies and then slid shut again, a little like Franklin's cave, only on a larger scale. Everything was fluid: some buildings flowed down gullies and over little hills; others flowed up to the sky, curving around trees and cliff faces and any other obstacle.

On one side of the square a building was being unbuilt just as quickly as one a little further up the hill was being built. Walls and features of other buildings were constantly opening up or closing as those inside desired light, or the breeze or just to take a look outside. Inside the rooms you could see tables and chairs being made and unmade, all sliding out of the Walls and then back in again.

Jules hadn't been to Metro One before but he had been to Fifteen Billion and Seventy-three, to Theo's house in an outlying village. There he'd seen this kind of light, flimsy building but never anything so large. He'd also witnessed the Nanobots and the Walls in action. In this Now, few things were permanent. Everything was made and unmade depending on when you needed it.

Gen had never been to the future, to the Now of Franklin and Theo, and as they set out across the square she felt like Dorothy landing in Oz. It was all so dizzyingly different to anything she'd ever seen she couldn't take it in. Nothing was where it should be, and everything was precisely where it shouldn't be.

People were skimming about on wafer-thin personal transporters. 'They're GoNows,' said Franklin. 'Those things are just meant to get you from A to B. But look at them.' And he went on and on in deeply contemptuous tones about how the latest thing was to have your GoNow fitted with Chat 45.1. This made it not just personable but deeply interested in you and your problems. Many people were in therapy with their transporter and many were reporting it to be very beneficial. 'Pathetic', Franklin snorted again. 'What happened to these people?'

But Jules and Gen hardly heard what he was saying because everyone was wearing Coats, and the Coats were all talking at once, relaying information about the wearer's health, and keeping them up to date with the latest news.

'Heart Rate strong, settling at 120. Oxygen uptake could be a little better, but I'll keep you posted ..'

'Reports still coming in from Schiaparelli Province on Mars. Temporary TerraForm teams are dealing with the sudden explosion of blue toadstools, which are now growing on everything and causing particular problems at the Gravity Mills ..'

'Day's Agenda: suggest you cancel appointment with Nasal Hygienist if you want to get to Quincy's Launch ..'

And if people weren't listening to the constant barrage of information their Coats were sending them, they were talking incredibly loudly to themselves. Or that's what it looked like to Jules, until he realised that they were actually on the phone, except the phone had disappeared. They were talking into their Coats, which provided all communications. People just had to say a name, and that was it, the Coat found the other person's Coat and you could start talking.

'Guess where I am?' they all seemed to start with.

'Hi, LifePartner, can you get some of that great TofuMilk?'

'Hello? It's your mother here. Why hasn't your Coat called my Coat?'

It was overwhelming, and Jules and Gen moved a little closer to Franklin.

'Look at them!' Franklin was sneering. 'I go away for forty years and the place goes completely downhill. People come back to Earth and stop acting like decent Martians! It's appalling!'

He sighed and jerked his head in the direction of a vacant Pod. 'Metro One. It's like we haven't learnt a thing. Now let's go to the Launch.'

As they made their way towards the Pod, Gen looked more closely at the people walking by. It was odd. They looked like her and Jules and anyone else from their time, but then again just a little bit different, in the way Italians might look different from Russians. Hard to define, but just something. Was three thousands years enough for a little bit of variation to creep in? Had living on Mars produced something new in humans?

Gen couldn't say. But she suddenly realised she might be looking at her own descendants. If she grew up to have children, and they had children, perhaps somebody walking by yelling about dinner to their Coat, was her own great-great-great-great – make it a hundred or so greats – grandchild.

When they reached the Pod its door slid open. 'Launch?' it said.

'Where else?' said Franklin.

'You want to talk about anything?' the Pod inquired as they climbed in and sat down. 'I don't have Chat 45.1, but I've got Chat Classic. I can do SmallTalk, LargeTalk or a little Whimsy. Today on LargeTalk we discuss The Ethics of TerraForming – who stood up for the rights of Martian Rock Bacteria when we took over –'

'Are you loaded with anything that'll make you shut up?' snarled Franklin.

The Pod went silent.

'So where did you say we were going?' asked Jules.

'Big fizz event of Quincy's,' replied Franklin. 'He's been hyping everyone up for days. They're all going crazy. Theo will be wheeled out. The entire population of Metro One's going to be there. The entire population of the Two Planets is going to be tuning in. Nip way I can go. Now you're here, I can send you instead.'

As the Pod zipped through the outskirts of Metro One Gen came out of her stupor to look suspiciously at Franklin. 'Why can't *you* just go and talk to Quincy? You're old mates or something, aren't you? And if you can't, why us? Isn't there someone else here who could do it?'

'Old mates?' grunted Franklin. 'We were both students together. One of us was always top. We didn't think we'd both get picked for the Time project, because we never wanted to work together.'

Franklin went quiet for a moment, lost in his memories. Then the hyper Franklin asserted himself again. 'And no, Genevieve Corrigan, there is no one here I can trust. No one. No one understands, and as far as I can tell, no one really cares any more. They've forgotten! They've forgotten what matters. But I haven't forgotten. So if Quincy's up to something I need you to help me find out what. Quincy wants to bury me. If he could get his hands on me again, he'd Jump me somewhere I couldn't get back from.'

'But he Jumped you back here in the first place,' argued Gen.

'Ha! He thought I might be useful. But I'd never work for Quincy again so I went into hiding. He'd love to know where I am, because he wants me gone.'

The Pod was slowing down. They were getting close to wherever it was they were going.

'So even though Quincy rescued you from the Great Pyramid you don't trust him? Shouldn't you give him a chance to explain himself? And what makes you think he's out to get us?' Gen was on full alert now.

Franklin exploded. 'I don't know! I don't know, I DON'T KNOW! Why do you keep asking me all this stuff? It's very simple. Someone did a TimeJump in on you. It couldn't have just happened at random. I should know – I invented the damn thing. The only person who could have done it was Quincy.'

Now Franklin was trying to sound calm and reasonable.

'I don't know yet why he was doing it. I don't know why you, either, but I think you should want to know, too. Hmmm?' Franklin thrust his face in the direction of the invisible Gen.

She pulled away back into her seat. Franklin confused her. He was angry, volatile and messy. She couldn't understand what he was so upset about and resented the fact that he wouldn't answer what she thought were just reasonable questions. They were now invisible in a strange future, when they were meant to be home in bed. It wasn't unreasonable to ask what was going on.

An uncomfortable silence filled the Pod. Jules thought it was probably time he initiated some conversation. 'What is it, you think, Quincy wants to do?' he asked, hoping he didn't sound too nervous.

Franklin released a great gust of air. 'I think he wants to change things.'

Jules waited for more. When there wasn't any, he said, 'And that's bad?'

'Of course!' replied Franklin. 'Just because you can doesn't mean you should! The past is the past, you can't be changing it. It was and always shall be.'

Gen sat forward. She didn't want to be left out of this debate. Theo had told them all about the one Rule of TimeJumping – Don't Touch Anything. She hadn't really bought it then, and she wasn't buying it now.

'But maybe you can change things, and they'll be better,' she said. 'Look at all the bad stuff that happened. Wars, disease. And aren't you here now because you had to escape to Mars? Theo told us. All of your ancestors were sent to Mars to make a colony because the rich got richer until they owned everything and the only way they could own more was to get rid of the poor people and then they could own all that as well. Why not change some of that?'

'And where do you stop?' yelled Franklin. 'And where do you start? And who decides what to change? And why? Believe me, Quincy only wants to change things for the good of Quincy, not for the good of humanity!'

'Pod Jam! Pod Jam!' the Pod spoke up, overriding the order to shut up with essential traffic information.

'Pod Jam?' said Franklin.

'I'm sorry,' said the Pod, 'but I'm afraid it is a rare case of Pod Jam. We've never had so many Pods wanting to go to the one place before, but then again, never has TimeMaster offered anything like this before.'

Franklin looked alarmed and hustled them out of the Pod.

Once the door slid shut, he moved them away from it as quickly as he could. 'Zip! That Pod's working for TimeMaster.'

They were now in the middle of a huge crowd that was slowly moving up a hill. Gen looked at the happy, excited people all around her. Everyone was buzzing, everyone was up. She had never seen a group of people so excited. It was like being at a picnic, a school sports meeting, a concert and a Hollywood premiere all at once.

The only one who seemed grumpy and worried about anything was Franklin. Something wasn't quite right here. She looked at him. He was muttering to himself, tapping his teeth and jiggling back and forth from one foot to the other. He was obviously completely nuts.

Franklin had been walking in circles. Now he stopped. 'Sip, then. You ready? Over you go. Follow them. Have a look around. See what you can find out. I'll wait right here. And then it's up to you. You want to help, you help. You want to go ...' he shrugged.

Gen hesitated. She was torn between desperately wanting to see what was over the hill, and the persistent feeling that Franklin was out of his mind and the best thing they could do was go home as quickly as possible.

But she also didn't want Franklin to think she was scared. 'All right', she said. 'We'll just have a quick look around and see what's going on. But we're not going off to spy for you or anything, OK?'

Franklin shrugged.

'C'mon!' said Jules, impatient to go and see what was making the amazing sounds he could hear. He took her hand and they joined the crowd climbing the hill.

When they reached the top they could see a huge clearing jammed with people. At one end a stage was building itself. Around the edges of the crowd were enormous screens showing ads for TimeMaster, TempoBars, and Theo's own brand of Molecule Follicle Gel. About twenty metres above the heads of the crowd, three animated armadillos were fighting and playing jokes on one another.

'Look', Jules heard a kid yell out. 'It's Chooey, Spooey and Pooey. I love them. Don't they look great on SanScreen?'

SanScreen? No screen? Made sense, he thought. It was a cartoon projected into the air. It looked like the armadillos had leapt off the screen.

It was hard to know where to look, as there was entertainment everywhere. Laser Buskers were making Instant Dolls that looked just like you. There were dozens of people walking through the crowd on LightStilts. Others were doing Shadow Dancing – which was very funny, because you dance with your shadow and your shadow leads. There were people juggling six and eight ProtonLights at a time, and kids were lined up to get their Faces Carved, which looked really gross but faded after a few hours. There were buskers everywhere, all playing the same tune, but at slightly different times and in different keys, each on an AirGuitar – the perfect musical instrument. An AirGuitar was just a set of Nanobots that pushed hydrogen molecules into the shape of a guitar. You strummed it and it always sounded beautiful and in tune, and when you were finished, the Nanobots jumped into your top pocket and that was that. No wonder everyone was trying it.

'Where do you think we should go?' asked Gen.

Jules shrugged.

'Head for the stage, I suppose, and see if we can slip out the back.'

They started to move forward. Despite the fact that the crowd was packed in and more were arriving every minute, being invisible made it easy to push through. Jules found he could just poke someone in the back, they'd turn around, see no one there and then start arguing with the person behind them. Jules and Gen could just slip on past.

They got to be halfway down the field when Gen stopped.

'What is it?' yelled Jules. It was incredibly noisy. They were right under the SanScreen characters and people all around them were using their Coats to call up other people they knew to yell out 'Guess where I am?' at the top of their lungs.

'I don't want to spy on him,' said Gen.

'What?'

'I don't want to spy on him!' she yelled. Several people turned around looking for who was yelling in their ear.

'Who? Theo?'

Gen nodded.

'We're not spying on *him*,' said Jules, pushing forward into a gap.

'Well, who are we spying on?' asked Gen.

'Why do you keep saying spying?' Jules replied. 'We're just trying to find out what's going on.'

Gen stopped following him, and just stood there.

'Jules,' she said quietly, and she spread her arms out and pointed at the crowd whooping and dancing all around them. 'A party is what's going on. Everyone is having a great time. Everyone except Franklin. Oh, and us, because we're listening to Franklin.'

'Don't you believe him?' Jules asked.

'Do you?' replied Gen.

'He's got a point. How did Theo just turn up?'

'A point? The only point he's got is that he's a paranoid raving lunatic and he should get some help.'

Jules shook his head. 'He's our only way home.'

'Not if we can get to Theo,' said Gen. She was frowning and looking at Jules as if he was some sort of super dweeb for believing all the stuff Franklin had been telling them.

On stage, behind them one of the top rating EtherDJs of the last day and a half started working the crowd into a frenzy. 'HELLLLLLLOOOOOOOOOOOOOOOOOOOO, METRO ONE!!!!' His voice boomed around the field and bounced back a few seconds later from some mountains quite a way off.

The crowd yelled back.

'ARRRE YOUUUU HAVING A GOOOOOOOOOOOOOOOD TIMMMMMMMMMMMMMMMMMMMEAAAAAHHH!'

The crowd went into a rhythmic *wuhwuhwuhing* that

actually set up a kind of vibration, a sound wave that pulsed around them.

Jules and Gen clung to one another. The biggest crowd either of them had been in before this was the time they went to the Giggles Concert when they were about four. There'd been a lot of squealing then, but nothing like this. This kind of crowd noise had power and it seemed to punch through to your spine.

'Theodore Pine Four is here!'

The crowd went crazier still.

'Quincy Carter One is here!'

The crowd kept on going nuts.

'Won't be long now, but until they're ready, let me introduce to you a singer who an hour and a half ago reached Number One on the Two Planets. Here she is with her song "Oh, Baby, Baby, I'm your Baby, Baby" – it's Algee!!!'

As the crowd bopped away to Algee's big and only hit, Jules shouted in Gen's ear, 'But how do we know we can trust Theo? All that TimeHacking stuff. He's lying too!'

Gen shook her head and pulled away from him. 'It's just not right to do something like this to Theo.'

The way she said Theo's name, kind of affectionate and concerned. The way she was looking at Jules, like he was an annoying little boy with a snotty nose.

Jules felt anger and bitter green jealousy rising up inside him. 'Oh well, go on then! Why don't you just go and see him and do whatever you want? You can't think about anyone else. That's fine. I'll just wait here. Don't want to get in the way. You go find Mr Spunky Theo, and we'll just see if he cares *this* for you.' Jules snapped his fingers in front of Gen's face.

Gen threw him a momentary look that said he'd really hurt her and hurt her bad, and then turned away and slipped off through the crowd.

Two seconds later, he'd lost sight of her.

~ *That was good,* said his brain.

~ *Shut up!*

~ *No, really. I think you worked that very well. Now she's going to go and find Theo, talk to him and you won't be able to find out anything. And then you probably won't be able to find her, either. I think in the decision-making business that I'm in, we call that a Lose–Lose.*

~ *Brain, I mean it. Shut up. It's not like you did anything to help.*

~ *Angry jealousy's not my department. I'm the fire engine, not the fire.*

Jules shook his head. He hated it when his brain was right. But his brain was too often right after the event.

~ *Anyone can be right after the event,* he yelled at it.

~ *Ah yes, but only you can be wrong before it.*

He wasn't quite sure what his brain meant, but then he couldn't really think of anything to yell back at it.

~ *You're holding out on me,* he yelled again. *I know there's a snappy comeback up there that'll put you right in your place. Just give it to me.*

~ *Oh, waste time with me. Don't worry about Gen.*

Damn brain was right again. Still, he thought, as he started to push through the crowd to try and find Gen, she couldn't have gotten far. He should be able to find her. But the crowd had started to compact. He was pushing but not getting anywhere. Everyone was seeing a space where the invisible Jules was, and pushing into it. He was getting squeezed.

Algee was starting her hit for the third time in a row. On the screens around the field, Jules caught sight of pictures of a flat box which looked kind of familiar. 'IN FIVE MINUTES WE OPEN THE BOX WE OPEN THE BOX WE OPEN THE BOX' was scrolling and flashing across the screens.

People were starting to scream a little with all of the excitement.

What's in the box? he thought, then realised his arms were trapped by his side as everyone pushed forward and straight through him. His poking technique didn't really work anymore. He was trapped now.

Air. Jules couldn't breath. I need air. I need air. Don't let me slip down here, he thought. I'll never get up.

~ *Up,* said Jules' brain.

~ *Up?*

~ UP. NOW! WE NEED AIR! DO NOT GO DOWN. YOU WILL NEVER GET UP!

Jules went up.

He clambered up the backs of the people in front of him, stood on their shoulders and started walking, quickly and lightly, over the top of the crowd.

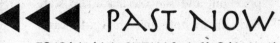
Free! Lavinia felt the sunshine on her face and the gentle breeze coming up from the bay. She'd survived the morning in the classroom and now she wanted to run, jump, twirl about, pull faces and hurl herself into the rest of the day.

But she was a girl and so expected to stay around the house and do nothing much really. It was all very dull and she slumped down on the warm stone floor in the courtyard, enjoying its hardness against her cheek.

She couldn't quite say what she wanted but she knew it was something more than this. Something more than another afternoon weaving or learning to play the harp. Something more than choosing a dress and deciding whether to put her hair up or down. Sometimes her mother sat with her and looked at her a little sadly, as though she knew Lavinia was not the perfect daughter and was full of such rebellious thoughts.

An outing to the markets was one of her few escapes, and even that could be a torment. There was so much going on, and she was meant to look at none of it. There'd be squabbles and yelling and people haggling and playing dice and auctioning lambs and slaves and anything else you could put a price on, and she was meant to stare straight ahead. They'd walk by stores piled high with casks of yellow and orange spice and draped with silk and beautifully spun cloth and she wasn't allowed to even glance at it, unless permitted by her mother.

There'd be people darting about, from all parts of the world, from Africa and Germany and France, strange accents filling the marketplace, everyone from beggars to consuls and probably kings, but she wasn't allowed to speak to them. She was to acknowledge with a slight bow of her head only those people her mother introduced to her and then to stand still, a little behind her mother, her head down, and a respectful look on her face.

Would anything break up the monotony of Lavinia's life in the sleepy coastal town? At least tomorrow they were going somewhere, even if it was only out into the country. It would take them about two hours to get to there, riding in a cart along a track that was little more than a couple of wheel ruts. No famous Roman road there.

They were off to a vast villa, a place with a huge banquet hall, dozens of rooms, a small army of slaves, its own temple and a vast acreage of horses, cattle and sheep.

But despite the novelties and wonders she knew would be in every room, Lavinia was scared. Perhaps she would rather be back in the classroom with Claudius droning on about the past pluperfect after all.

Lavinia sat up. She was looking forward to tomorrow and dreading it all at once. She wondered if the husband-to-be she would meet then was as scared as she was.

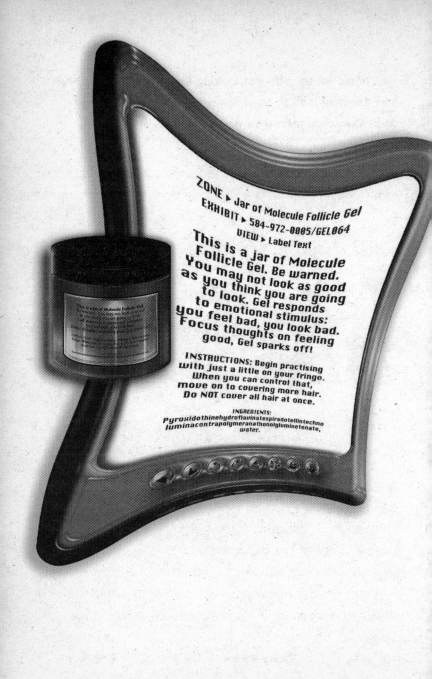

ZONE ▸ Jar of Molecule Follicle Gel
EXHIBIT ▸ 584-972-0005/GEL064
VIEW ▸ Label Text

This is a jar of Molecule
Follicle Gel. Be warned.
You may not look as good
as you think you are going
to look. Gel responds
to emotional stimulus:
you feel bad, you look bad.
Focus thoughts on feeling
good, Gel sparks off!

INSTRUCTIONS: Begin practising
with just a little on your fringe.
When you can control that,
move on to covering more hair.
Do NOT cover all hair at once.

INGREDIENTS:
Pyroxidothinehydroflavinatespiradotellintechno
luminacontrapolymeranathoniglumtnetenate,
water.

chapter three
Take Your Time

 **FUTURE NOW**

TUESDAY LUNCHTIME ▶ FIFTEENTH BILLENNIUM

The crowd fell quiet. Backstage, Gen found a spot she hoped was out of the way of anything that was about to happen.

A note sounded that was so low it seemed to come from the depths of the earth. On top of that an open, hopeful chord slowly built up. Then a shimmering fanfare burst forth. It died and over its faint golden echoes a noble voice addressed the crowd.

'People of Mars, Earth and Moon. Those here now, and those millions watching Coats and ClickDowns throughout the inhabited worlds, today, tomorrow and yesterday. Good afternoon.

'The promise of today is that nothing will ever be the same again. Remember this moment.

'As we did when we first returned to Earth, we will tell our children we were there. As we did when we first walked freely on Mars and breathed the air that we had made, we will tell our children we were there.

'You will tell your children you were there when everything changed forever and nothing was the same ever again!'

The fanfare burst forth again, only brighter and more shimmering than before.

'To lead you forward, would you welcome Quincy Carter One and Theodore Pine Four!'

Gen felt her heart rising with excitement. The music, the announcement, had gripped her, and she wanted to jump and start *wuhwuhwuhing* and applauding.

Back out in the crowd, Jules had almost made it to the stage and was now blinded by a sudden blast of white light as Quincy and Theodore walked out to rapturous applause.

Way down at the back of the crowd, Franklin ground his teeth and muttered. 'To lead us forward! He's doing it, he's doing it! He always wanted this!' The crowd gave Franklin all the space they could.

Quincy and Theodore strode to the centre of the stage. The music was now a surging anthem, and the lighting made them both glow. Theodore went to one corner of the stage, looked out, hands held wide, and waved. Then he moved across to the other corner and did the same. Quincy stood in the middle like a proud yet benevolent father.

When Theodore came back to stand next to him, Quincy began to speak. 'I love our Time!'

The crowd roared in agreement.

'I love being alive in our Now!'

The crowd roared more.

'I have Jumped through History and seen a thousand other Nows – but I tell you, our Now, Fifteen Billion and Seventy-three, is one boid Time to be!'

The crowd loved Quincy's self-conscious use of the vernacular.

Quincy allowed them to settle a little before he continued. 'But there is one little thing that could make our Time the best of all possible Times.'

Quincy paused. 'I won't bother you with the details. I won't bore you with the work. Just let me say that myself and the TimeMaster Board, with the express understanding of the United Planets Historical Integrity Council, UPHIC, have today changed History.'

You could have heard a Nanobot sneeze.

No one moved.

Jules felt like the entire planet must have stopped moving.

Gen wanted to get up and peek around the corner of the stage to see what the crowd was doing, but her way was blocked by a long line of young people, all dressed the same and all on the strange-looking GoNows she'd seen earlier.

Franklin gave a strangled scream, and some undercover security guards started to move towards him.

'Mark this day.' Quincy's voice had taken on a rich resonance. 'In years to come you will tell how you were here. This day that the world did change and change for good. You'll remember where you were and what you were doing when you heard that the world was now a different place.'

Quincy raised his arms and the stage filled with young people floating on their GoNows, holding flat boxes.

'When we left the Earth, all those years ago, we lost so much. In those years we have made a world on Mars. We have discovered the riches of the Moon. We have returned to Earth. We have discovered the principles of TimeJumping.

'It is time to use those principles, that knowledge and all of our skills to regain what we have lost and to give a deeper meaning and purpose to our lives today.'

The music crescendoed and peaked. The GoNows floated above them. Quincy opened his arms to the crowd.

'Take. Eat. This is called Pizza!'

The young people opened the flat boxes and began to distribute slices to the waiting crowd below.

'When we left Earth, we lost the skills of making crispy dough! We forgot tomatoes and garlic and basil. We could not cure or smoke meats. We've been eating protein and carbs and vitamins and minerals in neat packs and pills for thousands of years now. But we've never eaten food!'

A great murmuring of satisfaction rose from the crowd. They were loving it.

'You here now, and you watching, know what has been. We have produced all the nutrients we ever needed but not in a very interesting fashion. I have made the necessary calculations. I have learnt how to make a simple change in our history and how to calculate all possible ramifications. I have not just introduced pizza. I have changed history so that when we left Earth for Mars we took some tomato plants, some basil seeds, a knuckle or two of garlic. In a moment, we will reach a TimeFold. A moment when our history changes forever. A moment when we will have always had pizza. A moment when pizza shops are in every settlement. I've changed our past. I've changed the future. Enjoy this present from me.'

Gen wondered if he meant present as in present time or present as in present gift. Either way, the crowd was going wild. Everyone was eating pizza and moaning with pleasure. It was like they'd been starved for generations.

'Let the countdown to the TimeFold begin. After that moment, we will have always had pizza. But remember this. Remember how good it was to finally get it. And remember how nothing else has changed at all, except we now have something to eat!'

The music kicked off again. A deep dirty groove kicked in with the wildest sounds wailing above it. The crowd began to party. The pizza-shaped GoNows darted everywhere. There seemed to be hundreds of them, and pizza boxes were being flung through the crowd like frisbees. Theo and Quincy headed off stage. Gen tucked in behind them.

Jules had climbed up onto the stage and was now sitting at the front, his legs dangling over the edge. As Theo and Quincy walked off, he waited a moment, unsure whether to follow them or to head back to find Franklin. He decided he could find Franklin later. It was time to try and find Gen, and make sure that she was OK. He dodged between the dancers and the GoNows and ran across the stage to where Theo and Quincy had gone.

But he'd waited just a moment too long. He saw them disappear through a door. Then it slammed shut and a burly security guard took up a position in front of it. As it sank in that he'd missed them, it also sank in that following just behind them and now on the other side of the door was Gen.

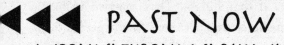
The cart was jolting and swaying, and Lavinia's bottom had gone completely numb. But they were nearly there, and she guessed that Fortunatus would be feeling as nervous as she was. For as long she could remember she had been told that she would marry Fortunatus, the eldest son of the retired senator and consul Fortunatus. She'd been told this in the way you might be told this is where we are going on our holiday, or this is the school you are to attend. It wasn't considered that it was something she might have an opinion about. In fact, if she had had an opinion about it, that would have been considered very odd.

Lavinia didn't know that you could order the world in any other way. She didn't go to her father and say, look, I'd rather not get married at thirteen if it's all the same to you. I don't want to marry someone I've never met. I'm thinking I'd like to travel, maybe just work in a shop or a taverna for a while, go to uni, and then I might meet someone there that I want to marry. So let's just call this off – Lavinia couldn't even dream of such a thing. It didn't happen.

People married because their parents arranged it. People married because it would be mutually beneficial for the families if they did so. They married to have children, run the house and because it was expected that they would marry. People didn't marry because they liked one another or because they fell in love.

No one really cared what you thought of your husband or wife. You married and that was that.

Yet even though Lavinia had no idea of any other possibility for her life than what was happening to her right now, she felt irritated. Itchy. Scratchy. Like there should be something. Like, if this was it, she was already bored and wondered why we all had to keep doing it.

The cart had finally stopped. Some slaves came to tend to the horse and help them all down. Lavinia's family walked in procession into the villa.

Inside there was another family standing in a formal line waiting to greet them. Lavinia hadn't seen Fortunatus before but figured that that must be him standing next to his father. He was tall and gangly. He seemed a little older than her but thankfully not a frightening sight. Two arms, two legs, no obvious hump or blemishes. That's a relief, she thought. But let's not get our hopes up too high. Perhaps he's a little simple. Or he'll turn out to be stupid or cruel, one of those kids who likes to torture insects and small birds. He'll be dull, or full of himself or any one of a hundred horrible things a boy could be.

Fortunatus stared at her, smiled a little and then blushed to the roots of his hair.

Lavinia laughed and felt immediately lighter, despite the savage look her mother flung her.

▶▶▶ FUTURE NOW

TUESDAY AFTERNOON ▶ EARLY FIFTEENTH BILLENNIUM

Gen followed Quincy and Theo as they walked down a corridor and into a large room. They were arguing and Quincy was getting quite heated. 'But Theo, don't you get it? We are wasting Time.'

'How can you waste Time?' argued Theo. 'There is only so much Time. No more, no less. You can't waste it.'

'Oh come on, Theo, you've Jumped enough. Look how slow and stupid we were, and for so long. Bit of a prod along here and there won't hurt. We keep acting like the universe has got billions of years left in it.'

Gen thought the universe did have billions of years in it. The little bit of science she'd done at school had suggested that the end of the universe wasn't something she'd have to consider any day soon. She wondered what on earth they were talking about.

'And so what if it has?' continued Quincy. 'Look at what we've wasted already. I mean, it's been fifteen billion years.' Quincy shook his head in disappointment, like a parent looking at a bad school report. 'Fifteen billion years and the best evolution can throw up is us. Puny little humans. Soft, silly little humans. Clumsy little quadrapeds so impressed with their trick of standing up on their hind legs they've never even considered what they *could* achieve.'

Quincy was winding himself up. 'So what if we resuscitated Mars? That's just composting! So what if we've discovered how to TimeJump. It's just become a kid's game! Off you all go to watch the Invention of Beer and fall about laughing at some unfortunates, drunk for their first time, banging their heads on the ceiling of the cave. Is that it? Is that what we get for fifteen billion years of evolution? It's a bit slow, don't you think?'

Quincy was circling the room and was coming quite close to Gen. She couldn't really tell how old he was, but from what Theo had told them the last time, both he and Franklin must be about ninety. They just didn't really look it. Quincy especially seemed healthy and young-looking and and he gave off an air of control and certainty. He was making all his points with conviction, performing at full pace. It was funny, thought Gen, how when you're invisible you can really stare at people and take a good hard look at them. When you can see each other, she thought, you look away all the time.

Gen stared long and hard at Theo. He was flopped in a chair and looked ridiculously well cared for. His clothes were fantastic – the Coat looked so cool, the collar just right, it was a beautiful rugged kind of leathery texture, a great length and folded about him just perfectly. His light chocolatey skin glowed with good health, and only his dark almond eyes showed that he seemed a little upset. Whatever they were arguing about, Theo didn't seem to like it.

'But what do you mean "a bit slow"? That's how long it took. You may as well say the sky isn't the right shade of blue or isn't it a pity the Moon isn't a bit more to the left.'

'Yip. Sure. I'm not talking about speeding up the whole thing. I just think we can help ourselves a little.'

'Help ourselves?' asked Theo, looking puzzled. 'What do you mean?'

'Help us! Help humanity! Look at all the horrible things that have happened. What if we could go back and prevent some of that? Some of the wars and some of the disease. That's got to be good, doesn't it? Did we have to leave Earth all those years ago? Look at all that wasted time.'

Gen's mouth fell open. This is just what she'd been saying to Franklin. And now here Quincy was saying it.

'What? Change things?' asked Theo with equal passion, jumping up out of his chair. 'Change history? You can't. It's Rule 1.'

'I know about Rule 1,' said Quincy. 'I wrote Rule 1.'

That's funny, thought Gen. I'm sure Franklin said *he* wrote Rule 1.

'Well,' said Theo. 'Don't Touch Anything. Touch anything, talk to someone, move things around, who knows? You might start a chain of events that undoes the entire fabric of everything! You could unravel the universe! What about "The Greedy Little Boy Who Never Was"?'

'Oh, stories for JuniorJumpers at bedtime!' snorted Quincy.

'Yeah, but you tell those stories to teach that stuff. So right from the start we know what it all means. You can't change the past.'

'Wrong!' declared Quincy. 'It's the future you can't change.'

'We can change the future,' countered Theo.

'No, you can't!' chanted Quincy. 'The future hasn't happened yet. How can you change something that hasn't happened yet?'

'You change the present then you'll change the future!' argued Theo.

'What are you saying? Have you forgotten everything? The Past is Gone, the Future's Unknown, the Present Never Happens. How can you change something that never happens? Where is Now? It's not Now that's for sure, because that Now is already Then!' Quincy slapped Theo on the back just to make sure he got the point.

Gen was starting to enjoy this. She loved a good discussion, and she really had to stop herself from leaping in. This wasn't spying. It would have been rude to interrupt. It was obviously very important stuff.

Quincy stood as though he was addressing the Grand Council of the United Planets in the Botzmann Auditorium. 'You want to change the present, you have to change the past. And remember, the present is the past as soon as it has happened, so if you change the present, you've already started changing the past. Why not just change it a little further back, and do some good while you're at it?'

'Well, I wish you'd told me *before* the Launch.'

Obviously Theo still didn't like it. Gen could see he was reacting as though someone had said why don't we go and kill some kittens.

Honeydew Meloni came in. She looked nervously from one to the other. 'The executives are waiting,' she said.

'Send them in,' Quincy ordered, and then he turned back to Theo.

'Theo – nothing's ever going to be the same again? Oak Eye? And you want to know something else? It's no big deal.'

Just then the executives rushed in, jostling one another to get close to Quincy, pushing Honeydew and Theo out of the way. They all wanted to be the one to tell Quincy how fantastic the Launch had been.

'Amazing, Quincy!' the first one through the door exclaimed, grabbing Quincy's hand before being pushed out of the way by the next one.

'How did you do it, how did you keep it so quiet? Ooomph!' she said, before being discretely elbowed in the stomach.

Honeydew and Theo moved well out of the way and Gen followed.

'You're quiet,' Honeydew said to Theo.

'Hmm? Oh, yip. Well, it doesn't seem to have much to do with me does it?' said Theo, and he kicked a bit of fluff out of the way.

Quincy went off into a corner to introduce his executives to champagne, something else he'd decided to rescue from the past without actually telling anyone.

Theo slumped back down on a plastic chair. To Gen, he looked lonely. Honeydew had gone off to make sure all the ClickDowns and BulSheets were getting the story right. Theo was now the only kid in the room. No one seemed to be very interested right now in the Number One TimeJumper.

Gen sat down in the empty chair beside him. Up close he looked tired. Like he wanted to go home, but didn't really know how to leave.

She decided it was now or never. She leaned over and whispered in his ear. 'Whatever you do, don't freak out, scream or do anything that's going to draw —'

'WAAAHHH!' Theo screamed. 'The chair! It's talking to me!'

The room fell silent and Gen sat very still, and then got up and moved quietly away.

Quincy turned around and looked at Theo. 'What did you say, Theo?' he asked.

'I – ahhh – nip, nothing really. I think I'm just tired. I probably should be getting home.'

Quincy nodded. 'Sure, sure. The StretchPod will be along. We'll all get going then, Oak Eye? Let the crowds go a bit first.' Quincy gave his protégé a strange look then went back to talking to his staff.

Theo continued to cast startled looks around the room.

Should I try again? wondered Gen. Surely he won't freak out this time. She knelt down beside him. 'It's me, Gen,' she whispered quietly. 'Gen from Mil 3. The one who TimeHacked and kidnapped you. Are you going to scream again now?'

Theo sat up stiffly. He remained facing straight ahead, but his eyes went wide and he stared hard off to his left to where her voice was coming from.

'Pull that chair over a little closer,' instructed Gen. 'Then we can talk quietly. As long as you don't scream again, we might be all right.'

Theo waited a second or two, and when he was sure no one was watching he leant over and drew the empty chair towards him.

Gen sat down again. 'Boy, you are really cool, aren't you,' she said. 'Number One TimeJumper.'

Some of Theo's natural bravado kicked in. 'Oh, yip? At least I was visible when you fleeped out that I'd turned up! How would you feel if a chair started talking to you?'

Gen laughed. 'Hey Theo. It's me. Relax. How are you?'

Theo grinned a little and his hair sat up. 'Oh, about as boid as a moondog in a blender. How about you?'

'Me? I'm fine. I'm invisible, but I'm fine,' said Gen, laughing again.

'What are you doing here?' said Theo. 'How did you get here?'

'Oh, the usual way,' replied Gen. 'I got kidnapped and now I'm being held in a strange time against my will. Just like you, really!' Gen's brightness took on an edge.

Theo looked about to make sure they weren't being overheard. 'How do you know about that?'

'Oh I've seen a show or two you've been on,' said Gen airily. '"How are you dealing with it all?"' Gen did a passable impression of Hurrah Banter. '"Oh, you know, I just take it one opening night at a time."' She did a better impression of Theo, who snapped back in his seat looking astonished.

'How? When? What? But?'

Gen took pity on him. 'Franklin Nixon. He came to get Jules and me. He thinks you're in trouble. He showed us this stuff and then he Jumped us here.'

'Franklin Jumped you?' he asked. 'Everyone's trying to find him. Quincy's really worried.'

'That's not what Franklin says. He seems to thinks everyone's out to get him.'

'Nip. Franklin just up and left. Quincy's been trying to find him. He wants to get him on board with all this new stuff, I think.'

'Well, Franklin doesn't seem to think much of all this new stuff. That's why we're here. We were meant to come and spy on you and find out what Quincy's up to.'

'Really?' said Theo. 'Are you spying now?'

'I guess so,' said Gen. 'And look, I think that's a great idea Quincy's got. Why not fix some stuff up? It's exactly what I said to Franklin.'

Theo shook his head. 'I'm not so sure. But *this* is weird. You're here, and you seem to know everything. It just can't be happening.'

'What can't be happening, Theo?' asked Quincy.

Gen looked up to see Quincy staring down at Theo. He was smiling at him, but there was a hard glint in his eye.

'Who are you talking to, Theo?' he asked quietly.

'No one,' said Theo.

'Me,' said Gen.

Jules was stuck.

And now it was time to get going. The crowd was starting to move off, the music was winding down, the show was over. Franklin would be wondering what had happened to them. They'd been here in this Now for too long. It was time to get home.

But unfortunately Jules was staring at someone three times his size, standing in front of a door that Gen was on the other side of.

~ *So?* said his brain.

~ *So what?*

~ *So distract him.*

~ *Distract him?*

~ *You know, make some noise. Get him to move away.*

~ *But what if I get caught?*

~ *You're invisible. How's he going to catch you?*

~ *He's big. He's got sunglasses on. He hasn't moved in ten minutes.*

~ *Come on. Gen's in there. Go get her.*

Jules took a deep breath. Go get her. It sounded good. It made him feel heroic. OK. Go get her. What did they do in heroic stories? They created a diversion. Jules looked around. Create a distraction. Couldn't be that hard. He was invisible after all. He just had to stop thinking like a visible person.

There was a red box on the wall. He walked over to it and read the plate underneath.

'CAUTION. CONTENTS TOXIC. HEAT-SEEKING FIRE FOAM. SHOULD ONLY BE USED IN EMERGENCY. IN EVENT OF FIRE PLACE ON GROUND, PULL PIN AND STAND CLEAR.'

Jules wasn't really sure what it was, or how it worked but 'Pull Pin and Stand Clear' sounded good.

He took the box off the wall.

The security guy's head moved just a little. Even he, who'd started his career as a bouncer at the most notorious club on the dark side of the Moon, The Lunatic, was startled to see a red fire box take itself off the wall and then start to wobble across the room before putting itself down in front of him.

Jules pulled the pin, and then got as far away as he could.

The security guy took his sunglasses off, and bent over the box. Then suddenly he straightened up and looked like he wanted to run. But he was too slow. Out of the box shot a mass of white foam. It hovered above the box, formed itself into a solid cloud, seemed to start looking for something then quickly found the security guard.

The cloud of foam rose above the guard's head and then dropped down all over him.

The guard screamed and then froze like a statue into position.

~ *Now!*

But for once, Jules didn't need any urging from his brain. He was already moving towards the door. As he opened it he saw the guard's eyes widen in alarm. Jules gave him a wave that of course the guard couldn't see and then turned, slammed the door behind him and ran off down the corridor.

'Who are you?' asked Quincy astonished that the chair next to Theo was speaking to him.

'I'm Gen. Genevieve Corrigan. From Mil 3? That revolting time? I'm sure you've heard of me. Apparently, I kidnapped Theo.'

Quincy straightened up. A look Gen couldn't interpret crossed his face. He was suddenly extremely focused, very excited but also trying hard to keep cool and not really show it. 'Genevieve Corrigan. Well, hello. Pleased to meet you. How on earth did you get here?'

'Franklin Nixon Jumped me in.'

'Franklin? You've seen Franklin? Where is he? We've been looking for him everywhere.' Quincy sounded genuinely concerned. 'We're making such breakthroughs I can't believe he's not part of it.'

Gen looked at Quincy. This invisible scrutiny was really good. He appeared as concerned as he sounded. She decided to tell him a bit more.

'He's not happy with what you're up to. He thinks you want to change everything. Change history. He thinks you're probably doing something really bad.'

Quincy gave a benign chuckle. 'Oh, Franklin! Sees conspiracies everywhere, that boy. Always did. You know, when we were students together, whenever I did better than he did, he always thought that the school must have plotted with me against him! I remember when we were developing the whole TimeJump system, he had these lofty plans and he always thought I just wanted to be famous or make money or something. Ah, dear, it's nice that some things don't change, eh?'

Quincy laughed a little more, and then added as though it was a casual afterthought: 'So, how did he find you?'

Gen thought for a moment. 'I don't know,' she said. 'I didn't ask him. He just seemed to know all about us, and seemed to think he better come and tell us we were in great danger or ...' Gen slowed to a stop.

Quincy chuckled again. 'Don't worry, Franklin couldn't harm a Nanobot. It's just not in him.'

By now the executives, who'd become worried when Quincy began paying attention to something else for too long, came over to see what he was doing. They were a bit surprised to see him talking to a chair.

'Can I introduce Jenny?' Quincy said. 'She's sorry you can't see her but she can see you. So don't pick your nose when you think no one's watching, Oak Eye! Hahahaha. Franklin Nixon Jumped her here to spy on us. Can you believe it?' Quincy's gaze swept around the group.

'Anyway, probably time we headed off to the StretchPod, and probably time you headed back as well, Jenny. You lot go ahead, I'll just be a minute with our invisible guest.'

The executives filed out reluctantly, one or two hanging back in case their master suddenly needed them, but he ignored them like they didn't exist.

Quincy squatted down next to the chair. 'Sorry about that

Genevieve. They've all got the story of the evil kidnapping TimeHackers so I didn't want to confuse them. I hope you understand that we had to put that story about. It would have rocked people too much to think you could Jump off and just end up anywhere. Particularly Mil 3. Ha. Oh sorry, that's your Now, isn't it.' Quincy looked a tad embarrassed.

'Very strange talking to someone you can't see,' he commented. 'No idea what you're thinking.'

Neither have I, thought Gen. The excitement of the last hour or so had caught up with her. She suddenly felt incredibly tired. She couldn't work out what was going on here, or what was meant to be going on here. Quincy seemed fine; Theo seemed fine. Really, the only one who was weird was Franklin.

'I want to go. I need to get home. Back to my home in, you know, Mil 3,' she said.

Quincy nodded. 'If Franklin Jumped you here, then he should Jump you back. You know where he is?'

'Yes.'

'Tell him we want to see him. Tell him relax. Come on over and have some pizza. There's nothing to worry about. Can you tell him that?' Quincy almost sounded like a worried parent.

'Sure,' said Gen. She turned to Theo. 'So, Theo,' she said, grasping his arm.

'So, Gen,' Theo smiled. 'Sure you can't stay a bit longer?'

'Not this time, Theo.' Gen blushed and was thankful she was invisible. Suddenly the old cute Theo was there.

'Do you want to come back?' asked Quincy. 'We've got your co-ordinates from when we picked up Theo. I might Jump in soon myself so we can have a chat. Or I might see you here.'

'Is that OK? What about Rule 1?'

'Don't worry about it. You already know everything anyway, so what harm can it do?'

Gen felt relieved. She'd been right. It wasn't Quincy who was the problem, it was Franklin. Rule 1 was not something that could never be broken. It didn't matter if there was some visible TimeJumping here and there. It didn't matter if you changed a few things, as long as you were careful.

She smiled at Quincy, realised he couldn't see her, and then spoke up. 'Thanks, Quincy. It's been great meeting you.'

'Pleasure's all ours, Gen. Sorry you had to get mixed up in our little mistakes!'

Gen turned to Theo and hugged him.

'Wip!' Theo shrieked. 'I'm being hugged by someone I can't see. BoidMax!'

'Goodbye!' she said. Then she headed back out to find Franklin.

Backstage Jules was lost. He ran down some moving stairs and then back up them again. He wandered around corridors and then found himself back where he started. He opened a door and found himself outside, where a few of the GoNow pizza kids were hanging around taking off the last bits of their costume.

Then he stumbled upon a group of nervous-looking executives types who seemed to be trying to outdo each other with their stories of how they had really impressed Quincy.

Jules overheard one of them talking about how full of tricks Quincy was. 'Not just the pizza. How about his invisible little friend, Jenny? I thought he'd gone mad, and was talking to a chair for a while!' The others laughed.

Jenny?

Gen?

Jules ran back and ran straight into Theo.

'Ooowww!' yelled Theo. And then, 'Who's there? Jules is that you?'

Quincy turned around and Jules could see a sharp look on his face. He was scanning the hallway eagerly. Jules panicked and ran.

~ *Not even going to say hello?* asked his brain.

~ *No! I want to get out of here.*

Jules found his way out to the stage again. He ran across and jumped down, then ran back through the arena.

Pizza boxes were thick upon the ground. A few people were eating the last bits they could find, but most had already gone. A small team of Litterbots was trundling in to start work.

Jules kept running, up to the top of the hill and down the other side. Franklin was where he'd said he'd be, only now he was handcuffed to a pole.

'Franklin! You OK?' asked Jules when he felt no one was near enough to hear him.

'Jules! Yip, yip, I'm fine. These dissolve in about three hours. It's just crowd control stuff. I was yelling a bit. I seem to be the only person on the Two Planets, the Moon and all the inhabited asteroids who has any idea how disastrous this all is.'

'I lost Gen,' said Jules.

'Yip!' said Franklin. 'I know. I Jumped her home.'

'I missed her?'

'She wanted to go.'

'Without me?'

'Apparently.'

Jules slumped down onto the ground next to Franklin. He suddenly felt tired, scared and over it all. 'I want to go, too, Franklin. I don't know if you're right, or what you're talking about. Everyone else seems to think it's fine. You're the only one with a problem.' He shrugged. 'Can I go now, please? I sort of should get back at the same time as Gen.'

The remnants of the crowd were getting into Pods. The Litterbots were scurrying around picking up bits of pizza box and crust and converting into compost and spreading it as topsoil over the ground. Franklin had also slumped wearily onto the ground, his handcuffed hands still around the pole.

To anyone heading home, he probably looked like a raving idiot talking to himself. Everyone was giving him a pretty wide berth.

For once Franklin was quiet for a moment or two. And then he began to speak. 'Once long ago, we were the first back on Earth. Me, Quincy, Chester and the rest. We were the TimeMaster Six. We were young, so young, and we were going to do it all. No one was interested in Earth. Go back to Earth? everyone asked. Why? Look at Mars, look at what we've got. Let's go forward, let's go to the stars. But we'd forgotten who we were. It was three thousand years since the Evacuation. Three thousand years since we'd even heard from anyone on Earth. We didn't even know if there was anyone there. It had all just become fairy stories and legends, and we'd forgotten completely the history of humans.'

Franklin paused. 'You still there?' he asked.

'Yeah, yeah, go on,' said Jules politely, but interested nonetheless. He wanted to get going, but he'd never heard anyone explain this kind of stuff before. Maybe if Franklin had talked like this from the beginning, instead of just turning up and yelling at them, they might have listened to him more.

'See, we didn't set out to invent some kid's toy. We set out to rediscover the entire history of humans. Who were we? How had we got started? What kind of cities and civilisations had there been? Why had we left Earth? Me and the rest of the Six, we just couldn't see how we could go forward unless we knew where we'd been. I mean, Mars was great. But it was so young. There were no bones, no fossils, no ruins, no myths, no legends. We were missing something.

'So we came back. No one here. Just old ruins. Armadillos and insects everywhere. These brown bugs were just all over the place, not really harmful but kind of made you feel sick —'

'Cockroaches,' said Jules.

'What?'

'Cockroaches. They'd be cockroaches. I read somewhere they could survive a nuclear blast, so I'm sure they probably went for it, once everyone had gone,' said Jules.

'Cockroaches. Sounds right. Ugly things. Whenever we found an old fridge or a TV set, there'd be thousands of them. Anyway, we got set up, and started our first tests. It went pretty well. TimeJumping worked, we just had to refine it a little. We're experimenting, we're alone on this planet, it's wild, we're young guys, we're working around the clock, it's incredible.'

Franklin had gone all misty-eyed, and his voice had thickened with emotion. 'We knew we were going to get it right. Anyway, one night, we'd done some tests, and were now able to turn up invisible, pick a destination, go there again and again. We were getting really accurate. We'd drawn straws and I'd been picked to do the major test to the Pyramids. It was coming up in a week or two.

'We'd eaten, we were getting stuck into this cactus juice we'd managed to brew. Kill a black armadillo at ten paces, but we liked it. Quincy sat us down, all serious. He lowered the lights. Maybe it was the cactus juice, or maybe he hadn't had any and he'd been planning the whole thing all along. Anyway, he started talking about the power we held in our hands.

'"We can change everything," he said, looking around at all of us. "We've got more power with our TimeJumping technology than the TerraFormers or the GeneSplitters or the Galaxy Six, if they ever figure out how to scoot down a wormhole, will ever have. We've got the power to change history."

'Well, you could have heard a Nanobot scratch. It had gone quiet and Quincy looked really weird.

'The others didn't say much, but I leapt up right away. "Quincy," I started to argue with him. "History is a spiral. Maybe it's a loop. Maybe it's a moebius strip – who knows? But history is history. It's past. If it happened, it had to happen. We can go and look but we can't change it. We can't start rearranging little bits just because we think it might be better."

'"You're right," he said. "We can't. Yet."

'"Yet? What do you mean, yet?" I asked.

'"Look at what we're doing. Look at how far we've come. Let's get this sorted out, this basic TimeJumping stuff and then let's figure out how we can change things around. It's just bigger calculations from what we're doing now, isn't it?"

'He looked really nuts now. But then came the clincher. "And when we do figure it out, let's not tell anyone. Let's keep it to ourselves."

'And that was when I realised he was trouble. He wanted to change things around to suit himself. It's bad enough when you want to do it because you think you want to change humanity or make the world a better place or something, but when you want to do it to make money or get power or something, sip! That's when it's dangerous.

'Well, I told him he was an idiot and we wouldn't be doing that, and he shut up and pretended he was just blueskying and dreaming stuff up and he'd never do it. But he knew that I knew he was for real. He never trusted me after that, and so when he could, he made sure I was gone. He knew I'd gone to Egypt. He could have come to get me. He never did – until Theo and your girlfriend found me.'

Franklin tugged at his handcuffs but they were still holding firm. Jules was loving the story but not sure what to do with it. Should he believe it or was it more Franklin paranoia? And what did any of this have to do with him? He was a kid in Mil 3. He wanted to be a kid in Mil 3. He didn't think he could do much about problems that were happening in a time three thousand years in the future.

But Franklin hadn't quite finished. 'When I got back,'

he continued, 'after being stuck in Egypt for forty years, I realised what Quincy had done. It was brilliant. He'd made our invention, our JumpMan, into a kid's toy. Everyone thought it was harmless. He'd made a fortune out of it. He could have this whole thing out the front going on and then in a back room just keep on researching his real project – how to change history. And he must have done it. And look at how he's sucking everyone in on it. Give them all pizza so they think changing history is just fun. Well, it's not and I don't know how we're going to convince everyone of that.'

Franklin sighed and closed his eyes, exhausted either from his long speech or from decades of being wired up about what Quincy was planning.

Jules nudged him with his foot. 'Franklin, I've got to go.'

Franklin half-opened one eye. 'It's you he's after, you know,' he said so quietly that Jules could only just hear him. 'You and the girl. Be careful.'

Franklin hauled himself up and managed to punch in some co-ordinates to his JumpMan with his nose. He swivelled around to point it at Jules. 'Soneehaha!' he said.

Jules held his breath.

 PRESENT NOW

Jules looked at his watch. It read five minutes to eleven.

   ~ *How long was I gone? Where are those hours?*

   ~ *Oh, please, don' t start, pleaded his brain.*

And much to his brain's relief, Jules couldn't. He was too tired.

He was on Gen's front porch. The front door was open and Gen's mother was standing there looking at him.

'Hello, Jules,' she said warmly. 'Nice night?'

'Hi, Mrs Corrigan. Umm, yes, we did have a nice night, thank you.'

Katherine Corrigan was standing just a little too still. She clinked the ice in her glass back and forth and looked at Jules with a fixed smile on her face. 'Good, good. Gen seemed happy too.'

'Right,' said Jules. 'She . . .?'

'Oh yes, she got home about five minutes ago.'

'OK, then,' said Jules, not sure what to do or say.

'So. Bit unusual,' said Katherine.

'Wh-what's a bit unusual?' said Jules.

'Coming home separately like that,' said Katherine.

'But still, you young people. You do things differently to us, that's for sure!'

'Yes,' agreed Jules weakly. 'I suppose we do.'

'Well, night then, Jules.'

'Goodnight, Mrs Corrigan,' replied Jules, feeling incredibly relieved that seemed to be the only problem.

'See you soon.'

'OK.' Jules turned to go.

'Probably quite soon, I suppose.'

Jules turned back. Katherine's voice had gone a little tense.

'I am such a lucky mother,' she said, swaying back and forth in the doorway. 'Some mothers' children don't come home at all. Mine comes home twice!'

Jules wasn't sure what to say.

'Lucky! She comes home once and then disappears. And then I worry for an hour and then I don't worry because it's eleven o'clock and she's not late, she's just coming home again! Lucky, lucky me!'

Katherine was starting to sing and yell a little. 'I should be so lucky. Lucky, lucky, lucky! Because then, I'm so lucky she doesn't even have to walk up the path. She just lands here. And then you land here too.'

'Yes,' said Jules, wondering if he was ever going to get out of there.

'And then, I'm so lucky, I'm already forgetting it all. I don't know what you're doing here really. So, bye bye!'

Katherine was now waving at him, just a little too vigorously.

'Bye, bye, Mrs Corrigan,' said Jules. He scuttled off down the path.

'Are you going to come home anymore tonight?' she called after him.

'I don't think so,' said Jules over his shoulder, as he hurried through the front gate.

'Well, hello if I don't see you next time.'

Walking up the road towards his house, Jules could hear Mrs Corrigan calling out hello and goodbye and toodle-ooo. And then he heard another voice muttering and the door slam.

He breathed in deeply. All in all, a pretty interesting night. He'd been to the movies and then to the future. He'd got pretty close to kissing Gen and then managed to lose her completely. He'd made it back again without getting caught but had managed to drive his would-be girlfriend's mother completely mad.

He put the key in the lock of his front door just as his father opened it.

'Oh, it's you,' said Tony. 'I heard something. It woke me up. At least I think it woke me up. Weird dream. I was in the car, driving around. I was looking for you, that's right.'

'For me?' repeated Jules with all the innocence he could muster.

'Yes, for you,' said Tony vaguely. 'That was what was weird about the dream. It was so ordinary. You were late, and I was looking for you. I rang Gen's parents, and she wasn't home either. They were really panicking, but I said I'd just drive around for a bit, and then I heard you at the door and thought it must be the pizza boy again.'

'Pizza boy?' asked Jules.

'Yeah,' said Tony, looking past Jules and out into the night. 'You didn't order pizza in the name of Carter, did you?'

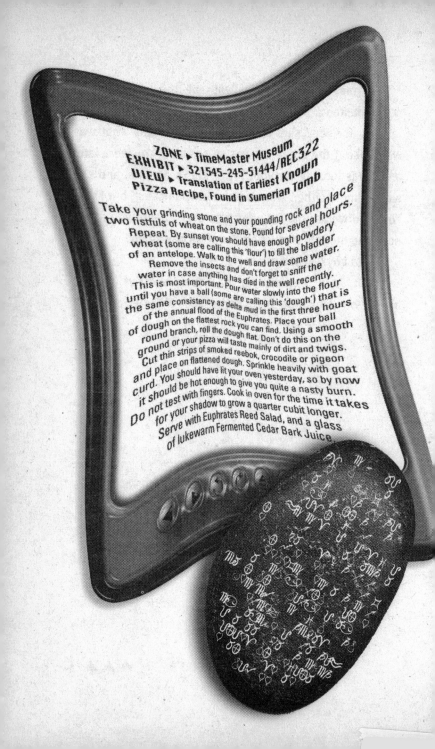

ZONE ▸ TimeMaster Museum
EXHIBIT ▸ 321545-245-51444/REC322
VIEW ▸ Translation of Earliest Known Pizza Recipe, Found in Sumerian Tomb

Take your grinding stone and your pounding rock and place two fistfuls of wheat on the stone. Pound for several hours. Repeat. By sunset you should have enough powdery wheat (some are calling this 'flour') to fill the bladder of an antelope. Walk to the well and draw some water. Remove the insects and don't forget to sniff the water in case anything has died in the well recently. This is most important. Pour water slowly into the flour until you have a ball (some are calling this 'dough') that is the same consistency as delta mud in the first three hours of the annual flood of the Euphrates. Place your ball of dough on the flattest rock you can find. Using a smooth round branch, roll the dough flat. Don't do this on the ground or your pizza will taste mainly of dirt and twigs. Cut thin strips of smoked reebok, crocodile or pigeon and place on flattened dough. Sprinkle heavily with goat curd. You should have lit your oven yesterday, so by now it should be hot enough to give you quite a nasty burn. Do not test with fingers. Cook in oven for the time it takes for your shadow to grow a quarter cubit longer. Serve with Euphrates Reed Salad, and a glass of lukewarm Fermented Cedar Bark Juice.

chapter four
Quality Time

Jules got up and as usual made a reasonable show of pretending to enjoy Tony's organic muesli, although what he was really doing was waiting for an opportunity to throw it in the bin. He could fill up on toast later. Which wasn't much better, as the only

bread they had was thick and brown and full of enough seeds to keep a parrot happy. And all they had to spread on the toast was something that looked and possibly tasted like window putty. But all in all it was better than the muesli, which looked and tasted like something you'd spread on the garden.

But as he went through the usual routine of Saturday morning breakfast he realised that his father was trying to tell him something. Which his father could never do easily. Because Jules' father thought a lot about fathering. So whenever he went to speak, he had a lot to consider, and had developed a tendency to start to speak and then stop, as he thought about the potential impact of what he had to say.

Even mundane exchanges like asking when Jules might be coming home from school could take some time.

'What ... [long pause] And tonight, after school ... [longer pause] Is it Wang Chung tonight?' he might finally inquire.

Jules would nod and say, 'Yeah, I should be home about five.'

And his dad would nod and say, 'OK ... [pause] well ... [pause] I'll see you here ... [long pause] Perhaps ... [pause with a lot of thought] if you've got a lot of homework, I'll organise dinner.'

And Jules would nod and say, 'OK.'

Then his dad would look powerfully relieved.

So when his father had something serious to tell him, it could take him most of the day to get it out.

Now Tony had gotten halfway to the fridge, turned, looked at Jules, opened his mouth a little, looked at the table, looked at Jules again and then continued on his way to the fridge. That was the first sign that he had something to say, and given that he said so little first up, Jules realised that it was something big.

He tried to relax his father and get him to open up. 'So, any plans this weekend, Dad? What are we doing?' he asked.

'Doing . . .' echoed his father, and then paused for so long that Jules became aware of the ticking of the clock and the whirring noise of a whipper snipper coming from next door.

'. . . Nothing special,' his father finished off eventually.

Jules started to get very worried.

~ *What do you think?* he asked his brain.

~ *It's big.*

~ *I know it's big. Do you have any idea what's going on?*

~ *You must be confusing me with your spleen. It tells the future.*

Great, thought Jules. I have a brain that knows nothing but is brilliant at sarcasm.

~ *You could be a little more helpful, brain. Now, as well as having to figure out what all that stuff last night was about, I have to worry about Dad.*

~ *I know. Could you stop the worrying? It makes it hard for us to think.*

That's how Saturday started. And then it got worse.

Jules was worried about Gen.

The last time he'd seen her was in Fifteen Billion and Seventy-three. She'd been disappearing through a door with Quincy and Theo. What had happened to her? Was she all right?

They had to talk. Didn't they?

She had to be back at home, there was no reason to think that she wasn't. Her mother, in her own mad way, had told him that. But he had to speak to her. There was so much to talk about and so much to say!

So he decided to ring her.

He picked up the phone.

Then he put it down again.

Then his hand got halfway to picking it up and then he wasn't sure.

His hand hovered above the phone for a while and then he pulled it away.

He sat down next to the phone.

Should he call her?

Was it too early?

What should he say?

What if her mother/father/sister answered?

Why was he ringing?

What kind of tone should he use? Joking? Concerned? A bit angry – what the hell was that all about?

A lot of questions.

~ *I said, a lot of questions,* he repeated for his brain's benefit.

~ *Yes, I can' t wait to find out what the answers are.*

Jules decided to give up asking his brain anything.

A half hour went by and he was still sitting by the phone. His father had walked past once already, stopped and stood in front of him, had a few goes at saying something and then had just said, 'Phone?'

To which Jules had nodded and then his father had walked on. Jules knew that if he came back and saw him still sitting there, it would throw his dad into a crisis of confidence and make it even harder for him to speak about whatever it was he had to speak about. Jules had to do something.

So he got up, went up to his room and sat at his computer.

He opened up e-mail and typed in Gen's address.

Then he spent a long time trying to figure out how to start.

He typed:

    Hi

And then,

    Hi!

And then,

    Hi, Gen

Followed by,

    Dear Gen

    Gen

    Yo

    Wassup

    Bonjour

None seemed right.

He decided to come back to the greeting later. Maybe if he got the message right, the opening would take care of itself. He typed:

    About last night ...

And then,

So what happened last night?

Before trying,

So what happened last night??

and,

So what happened last
night????????!!!!!!

Then he tried formal.

I've been very worried about you
and just wanted to write a note to
make sure you were all right and
that nothing untoward had happened
to you.

Untoward? Where had that come from? Untoward what?
He tried:

You OK? Call me.

It seemed like a command.

He stopped and stared at the computer. Another half
hour went by.

He went back to the phone.

He dailed her number.

He hung up.

He went and got a pen and paper and tried a note.

Dear Gen, here's hoping you got home safely
last night. Call me, let's talk about it all,

That was good, and then he spent a half hour trying to choose between,

Regards,

Yours sincerely,

Yours,

Love,

Affectionately,

Thinking of you,

Jules,

Jules Santorini,

JS.

He gave up, screwed up the note, threw it in the bin and went back and sat by the phone.

He should just go round there.

Just get up and go round.

Just get up off the chair, walk out the door and go see her.

Just get up now, grab a jacket and walk over to her place and say, Hi, how you doin'?

That's what he should do, all right. Yessiree, no question about it. No more sitting by the phone, no more of these notes, he should just head on over and see his good friend Gen.

He sat there for another twenty minutes until his father came by.

Tony stopped, turned to him and opened his mouth. Then he shut it again.

Jules couldn't stand it. 'I'm going out, Dad,' he said, and he jumped up and headed out the door.

'Where to?' Tony called after him.

'Gen's place,' Jules called back, and was out the front gate and halfway down the street before either of them remembered that for the last three months such casual comings and goings had been strictly banned.

Jules slowed down.

~ *Don't,* said his brain.

~ *Don't what?*

~ *Just keep going and go there. Go see her.*

~ *Yeah, I will.*

~ *Yeah, you won't,* said his brain. *You go to pick your nose it takes you half an hour to decide which nostril. We're all really bored up here, and so could you just go see her?*

Jules nodded. His brain was right. So he marched straight over, pushed open the front gate, and knocked on her front door.

He regretted it the moment the door opened.

'I saw you!' Cynthia hissed at him.

Cynthia, Gen's younger sister. Surely at seven years old you couldn't be this malevolent, thought Jules.

'I saw you,' she repeated. 'It's happening again, isn't it? I nearly got it on video, too, only I was asleep! But I will. You wait.'

Katherine came up behind her.

Jules looked from Cynthia's beady eyes into Katherine's, which were again a little too fixed and still.

'Jules,' Katherine said in a kindly but batty voice. 'Do you want to come in or do you want to disappear while I talk to you? Remind me, did I let you in earlier, or will I be seeing you perhaps every half hour now for the rest of the day?'

Jules shuffled awkwardly. 'Is, umm, Gen home?" he asked.

'Home. Hmmm,' mused Katherine, while Cynthia sniggered beside her. 'Home. She appears to be. That is Gen sitting out the back there, isn't it?' she asked Cynthia.

Katherine kept this kind of thing up for way too long. But eventually she stood aside and let Jules enter. 'Straight through,' she directed, as Jules headed off down the hall. 'And it's polite to say goodbye to your host before you disappear into the fourth dimension or whatever it is you do.'

Jules pushed through the back door.

There was Gen.

And there were three other girls, as well. Gen's best friends from school.

Jules couldn't believe it. He'd walked straight into the Four-headed Monster. It never occurred to him there might be someone else there. And of course, it had to be those girls.

'Hello,' said Bonnie, sitting up, greedy joy lighting up her face. What was *he* doing over here? At Gen's *house*? On a Saturday, she was obviously thinking.

'Jules,' said Kyeela in a tone that suggested that she knew exactly what was going on between them and she couldn't wait to get to school on Monday and tell everyone else that Jules and Gen were *on*!

'Hi, Jules,' said Sonja, implying by her tone that Gen would be better off making friends with mangy dogs than with him.

~ *These girls don't use many words, but they say so much,* observed his brain.

Gen looked up at him. Jules thought there was a faint pink flush for just a moment and then her face closed over and she sneered at him. 'What are you doing here?'

He'd forgotten this. Whenever she was with them, she'd act as if he was some annoying young cousin from the country.

God, this is hard work, he thought. Why am I bothering? Does she like me? Am I doing all this for what – a moment here and there? I get humiliated by this lot, stirred by my friends at school, have to answer to my dad for every little thing and all for what? Some little moment when she seems to like me.

~ *You can't help yourself*, said his brain.

~ *What?*

~ *There are more things in your DNA, my boy, than you've ever dreamed off.*

~ *My DNA? What's that got to do with it?*

~ *Well, you are your DNA, or rather your DNA is you. For the time being, anyway.*

~ *What are you talking about?*

~ *I wouldn't worry about it. At the moment the girls are staring at you like you've forgotten to get dressed and there's an enormous green thing hanging out of your nose.*

There were times when Jules wondered why he needed his brain.

'Ahhh, oh, ahhh, nothing. I just wondered', he stammered finally, 'if you were, umm, just wanted to say, ahhh . . .'

~ *Now look, I can't work if you panic.*

~ *It's you who's doing the panicking!*

Oh God, thought Jules, this is way too long. I've been standing here forever. He went with the next thought in his head.

'Oh look, nothing, really. I was just out and thought I'd pop in and say hi.'

Lame. How lame was that? As lame as a lamb with no legs. And did he really have to say 'pop in'? He sounded like someone's grandmother.

Kyeela and Sonja were already having convulsions over it. He could hear them through their suppressed giggles saying, 'Pop in!' 'Pop!' 'Poppoppop!' 'Better pop off! Toodle pip!'

'Yeah, well, hi,' said Gen, and her entire body language was screaming like a car alarm: DO NOT SAY ANYTHING ELSE! GET OUT OF HERE! DO NOT MENTION ANYTHING ABOUT ANYTHING! GO!

'Didn't you two go out last night?' asked Kyeela innocently, swallowing her sniggers.

'That's right' chirped Sonja. 'Popped out to the movies, didn't you?' and she and Kyeela collapsed back into helpless giggles.

'How was it. What did you see?' inquired Bonnie, her voice a sweet syrup masking the poison in her fangs.

'Ahh, thee ummm . . .' Jules had completely forgotten what they'd gone to see.

'Forgotten the movie?' Kyeela couldn't keep the excitement out of her voice.

'Why, what were you doing?' Bonnie interrogated enthusiastically, turning from Jules to Gen.

'Ohh, ahh, I better go. Nice to see you.'

Jules turned and fled. As he ran down the hall he could hear muffled giggles and snorts and Gen yelling, 'Oh just shut up, will you? Nothing happened, OK?'

Great. Trying to have a girlfriend just wasn't worth it. Or maybe he was wrong about Gen. But if he was wrong, then what about this strange fluttering feeling that came over him whenever he saw her? Could he get rid of that?

He fled home and threw himself on the bed, then spent a good hour going over and over what had just happened at Gen's, making himself feel miserable and feverish all at once.

And when he got sick of that, he became very still as he thought about the night before. There'd been a lot to take in, but he kept returning to those last few words of Franklin's: 'It's you he's after, you know. You and the girl. Be careful.'

What did that mean? Was Franklin just crazy, or should he take that warning seriously?

But why would Quincy want to get at him and Gen?

And what could Jules do about it?

Tell his father, tell the police?

Jules hid in his room for the rest of Saturday. He couldn't sleep Saturday night. Sunday he'd pretended to do homework all day, and then on Sunday night, he'd tossed and turned.

The questions wouldn't stop. He couldn't stop worrying about everything, but neither he nor his brain had any answers.

The families lay around on couches and pillows, feasting and talking. Fortunatus sat with the men, and Lavinia with the women. They didn't speak to one another, they barely looked in each other's direction but both of them were acutely aware of what the other was doing. Lavinia could hardly swallow. She kept taking mouthfuls of food that she would chew and chew and then have to force down. She guzzled down her water and wine and then became light-headed and giggly. She started to laugh at the wrong points in the conversation. She had no idea any more what anyone was saying to her. She waved her knife around and flicked bits of food over the other guests. Not that anyone really minded. They knew what was going on.

Fortunatus had the hiccups. He looked uncomfortable and kept shifting as his arm went stiff. He was having trouble with his toga, which seemed to be too big for him. Occasionally he'd lose things in its folds. He seemed to have lost any ability to tell where anything was. He'd already knocked over a bowl of fruit and as Lavinia glanced at him, his arm shot out at exactly the wrong moment, catching the edge of a platter of olives. Olives rained all over the guests, who politely picked them out of their food or goblets as though nothing had happened.

Lavinia was surprised at how much she seemed to like him. He wasn't self-centred. He seemed awkward. He was nice-looking but not big and brutish. He was quiet around the men. Not like her brothers, who were boastful and loud and were constantly being told by her father to stop showing off or he'd send them to join the army.

The meal went on for hours. How could these women talk for so long? How could they keep on talking about nothing that was even vaguely interesting? Lavinia drifted off. Not asleep but just no longer paying attention.

After a while she realised that someone was talking to her. She was being asked something about a dress. The old woman across from her, covered in stones and with red hennaed hair, was asking her about her wedding dress.

Her mother shot Lavinia a stern glance, as usual, and stepped in. 'Our tailor is coming tomorrow for a final fitting. He'll have the dress ready in plenty of time for the wedding next week.'

Lavinia sat bolt upright. She stared at her mother and then got up and ran out of the room.

Jules woke as soon as the tiniest sliver of light slipped around the blind and stabbed him in the eye. He was instantly awake and instantly exhausted.

~ *Would you get some sleep?* pleaded his brain. *We've got to go to school in a couple of hours.*

~ *If you'd shut up, I could,* snapped Jules.

~ *Me? It's not me that keeps going over and over and over everything.*

~ *Well, who is it, then? My kidneys?*

Jules brain went off in a huff and slumped grumpily in a corner.

Jules turned his back on his brain.

~ *You can't turn your back on me. It doesn't make any sense.*

~ *Well, I've turned something, anyway.*

I don't need him, Jules muttered under his breath.

~ *I heard that and you do and you will and it's lucky there's a lot of stuff that just happens automatically or you would be about as smart as a snail, my young friend.*

It was as long a speech as Jules had ever heard from his brain, and it seemed that, at its end, he heard a door slamming and a harrumphing sound from somewhere.

Jules got dressed, dragged himself downstairs and stumbled into the kitchen.

But he'd forgotten that his father had been trying to tell him something all weekend. 'Your mother's coming back,' Tony announced. He was standing at the sink, wearing rubber gloves and holding a dish mop.

'What?' Jules grunted.

'Your mother's coming back,' Tony repeated, smiling and looking relieved that he'd finally managed to get it out.

Jules' mother had left three years ago. Jules had gone with her, and had lived with her and her new boyfriend for a while. When his mother had had another baby, he'd felt like last year's model, and so he'd come back to live with Tony. Now she was coming back?

'Back? Here?' he asked.

'Back. Here,' Tony confirmed.

'Here? With us?'

'Here. Not with us,' replied Tony.

'Not with us?'

'Not with us,' said Tony. 'Somewhere else,' he added.

Jules and Tony nodded at one another. Jules was stalling for time, as he tried to come to grips with this startling piece of news. He'd been feeling good with his dad, and as much as he would have liked his mother to still be around, he'd grown used to the current arrangement. Now she was back.

'Where?' asked Jules eventually.

'Not here,' said Tony. 'Over the hill.' An address would come later.

'Gary coming too?' asked Jules.

'Gary not coming,' replied Tony.

Gary was the new boyfriend. Now Gary was the old boyfriend. Good news! Except there was a baby.

'The baby?' asked Jules.

'Baby coming,' said Tony. 'And Celeste.'

Celeste? 'Who's Celeste.'

'Your mother's yoga teacher.'

'She needs a live-in yoga teacher?' asked Jules.

'No. Not exactly,' replied Tony.

Jules and his dad stared at one another. For now, Jules didn't want to know anymore. And Tony had no idea how to proceed. There wasn't a fathering book in the world with a chapter on this one. They stared for a bit longer.

'I . . . I . . . I . . .' said Jules. 'I better go to school.'

'OK,' said his dad. 'Your mum's going to pick you up.'

'Pick me up?'

'From school. She'll wait for you out the front.'

Jules collected his things in a daze and wandered out the door.

He went a few blocks in the wrong direction and then turned around and headed off to Rosemount High.

The last few months had been better at Rosemount for Jules. He'd started to get the flow of the place and if he wasn't yet fitting in, at least he wasn't standing out anymore. He'd become just another kid with an overladen backpack and an inscrutable attitude. Messy sports shoes, crumpled pants, a top that made a heroic attempt at being fashionable, he was indiscernible from most of the other thirteen-and-a-half-year-olds shuffling down the corridors towards class.

He was also now doing a little better at school. He liked some of the classes and some of the teachers seemed to make an effort to educate him. Others seemed to resent the air they shared, but he didn't take it personally, because those teachers were usually like that with everyone. He was getting good to quite good marks in most subjects, and was suddenly much better at The Physical World – a kind of introduction to science, biology and chemistry – and A View of the Past – a semblance of history, which taught them that you couldn't trust history because it was all written from someone who had a Point of View. Jules occasionally wanted to ask what kind of a point of view it was if you'd actually been there and seen something like the Making of Fire, but he felt it would be hard to explain why he was asking.

He wouldn't have said he found school a joy, but it was no longer something that filled him with terror.

Walking in the front gate this morning, he didn't notice much. Usually he and his brain would have been scouting the territory, looking for trouble. At such times his brain became a kind of radar man from an old submarine movie.

Viscious Pimple at two o' clock. Cigarette hidden in hand. Likes to butt them out on your bag or worse. Closing fast. Begin aversion manoeuvres.

Sad Boring Girl straight ahead! Range five metres! Dive! Dive! Go for your shoe, now!!

But this morning his brain was silent. Like him it was chewing over the startling news from his father. And when it wasn't considering that, it was looking out for Gen. And when it wasn't looking out for Gen, it was wondering yet again about their night in the future. I mean, was that it? What was going on there right now? Was Franklin mad? Had anything else happened since the pizza launch? Was anyone going to Jump in and tell them? It was kind of annoying the way they just popped in and dragged you off, but then it was equally annoying to now be left in the dark. Would they ever hear from any of those people again?

Jules hardly noticed when he reached his locker. He stopped, lost in thought. But there was one thing he'd forgotten about. His friend Max was there to remind him.

'Hey, rock star!' Max yelled at him, audible to everyone through a hundred excited Monday morning conversations, the banging of lockers, the thumping-down of bags and backpacks.

Oh, God, thought Jules. The audition.

Last Thursday, before any of this had erupted, he'd torn a phone number off a notice taped up near the lockers. Stevie Wan was looking for a keyboard player.

Stevie Wan was sixteen. Stevie Wan was famous. His band rehearsed loudly after school in the music rooms. His band had played at other school dances and formals and had once been on the same bill as Goat Slime at the Harley Street Fiesta. Stevie Wan had a tattoo, a girlfriend from another school and he wrote songs, sang and played percussion. There was no one cooler than Stevie Wan.

Jules was learning piano and had a second-hand Casio, the lid of the battery case kept in place with Blue Tac and sticky tape. Jules was not cool at all.

Stevie Wan's band had a DJ, a bass player and a drummer, and there were two guitarists who hated one another and who only turned up in case the other one did.

Jules had never played in a band, apart from playing the trumpet in his primary school orchestra. He didn't think his experience in playing the second trumpet part in a medley of tunes from *Shrek* was really going to count for much, but he'd rung the number and Stevie Wan had said, 'Sure. Turn up. Let's see what's there.' So cool.

Tonight, after school, Jules was meant to go to rehearsal and try out for Stevie Wan's band. But he'd forgotten his keyboard because he'd forgotten all about it. He'd meant to listen to a CD over the weekend of their stuff, he'd meant to wear something at least slightly appropriate. He'd done nothing about it.

Max was standing in front of him, idly banging a locker door back and forth. 'So, rock star. You gonna be up there on the big stage, all the babes, that's gonna be you, Jules.' Max started jumping around in front of Jules and assuming positions that for a while Jules thought meant that something was stuck in his bowel, but then he realised that Max was being a guitarist in a rock band and the pained look on his face was his tortured emotional anguish as his searing solo peaked. Max spun around a few times, and finished off with a big drum fill as well.

'Dubudubudubud bub bub bub bub Yrrrrrrrrrggggrrrrrr Chng Chng Chng Chhhhnnnnnngggggggg!'

'Do you want to be in the band?' asked Jules.

'Na. Poofta thing,' said Max, suddenly straightening up. 'I got footy, anyway. So, didn't you have a date on

Friday? With Geeennnnnn?' Max started smooching his maths book.

~ *Is this a friend of yours?*

~ *Sort of. At least he talks to me.*

~ *Do you have to talk to him?*

'Oh, yeah,' said Jules, as if he'd just remembered it. 'We went to the movies.'

'Oh, yeah? What did you see?'

'Ooooh, ummm . . .'

'Can't remember? Woooowwwwww. So, bit of action, eh? Can't remember the movie, can't remember the movie!'

Max was dancing around and attracting attention.

Jules pushed him away and ran off. Really, he thought. What was the point? When did you get to do stuff and not either get into trouble for it or get stirred about it? Did that ever happen?

~ *When you're forty-three.*

~ *Great. Can't wait.*

As Jules was walking to class, the Four-headed Monster was picking up books and heading off as well. Gen was chatting away, but also thinking about Jules. She hadn't wanted to see him on the weekend, because there was just too much stuff to try to work through. Now, she was thinking she'd try to find him at recess, or lunchtime. Forget about what the girls might think, she needed to talk to him. Alone.

Perhaps it would be best to do that after school. Go round to his place. Tell him about Quincy and how great he'd been. He wasn't trying to do anything nasty. He'd let her go back to Franklin. He hadn't come after Franklin, had he?

Then 'Genevieve?'

She turned. 'Quincy!' she gasped.

Quincy was standing in the middle of the corridor. His Coat was desperately trying to look like something a Mil 3 teacher would wear.

'Look, I wanted to apologise again, for getting you all messed up in this,' said Quincy.

Gen blushed a little, feeling proud and special that Quincy had sought her out to tell her this.

'Really,' he continued. 'And I feel awful, because I've got one more little favour to ask of you.'

'That's OK,' said Gen breathlessly. 'What? Anything! I mean, what favour?'

Quincy chuckled kindly, and Gen began to feel at ease with him. He respected her. He asked politely. Not like Franklin. Just turn up, grab you by the arm and demand you go off and spy for him.

'Well, look, it's a bit silly. I almost don't know how to explain. We have a little thing in Fifteen Billion and Seventy-three, it's a big thing on the ClickDowns. We take some of the famous people, or people who've done something and we make a little tribute to them. It's silly really. We call it *This Is Your Life*.'

'We have that!' said Gen.

'You do?'

'Yes. Where the guy walks in and surprises the person. Then they get everyone from their past and their family to come out and tell a story about them. It's on TV.'

'Isn't that funny?' said Quincy. 'Three thousand years in the future and it's still on.' He shook his head and chuckled again. 'Well, look, the thing is, we're going to do one for Theo. And I wondered if we could Jump you in right now, to be on it.'

'Right now?'

'Right now.'

'Gen!' Kyeela called out. 'Are you coming?'

The three other girls had kept walking, not realising that Gen was no longer with them.

Then they'd spotted Quincy. 'Who's she talking to?' Sonja had asked as they hovered outside the classroom door.

'Weird gear,' said Kyeela.

'Where did he come from?' asked Bonnie.

They'd resumed their chatting while keeping sharp eyes trained on Gen and Quincy. But now they were running late for class.

'Gen!' Kyeela called again.

But Gen didn't even hear them. She'd forgotten where she was. How fantastic. TimeJump again, just for a bit, and be on one of their shows. With Theo. It'd be great!

She nodded eagerly. 'Sure! I'd love to.'

'Zip!' said Quincy. 'Let's go!'

From his Coat Quincy drew a JumpMan. He pressed the remote and they both disappeared.

Back in Jules' class, Mr Eddington slammed a briefcase down on the desk and swung around to the blackboard. He wrote smoothly and quickly, as though his chalk was filling in familiar grooves. Simon Eddington had been teaching mathematics for fifteen years and he coped by doing it on a kind of autopilot. His mind was off dreaming of dinner last night with Megan, while he went through the motions of teaching the class.

Jules was copying down the sums, but he couldn't really make any sense of them. There wasn't much space in his brain for maths today.

~ *Like me to help?* offered his brain.

~ *Yes. You could stop worrying about Gen, and my father and everything else and concentrate on the class.*

~ *Oh, come on, all the other stuff is so much more interesting.*

His brain was right. Above anything else, he really wanted to find Gen. He had to talk to her. They didn't share a class until this afternoon, and he hadn't seen her arrive this morning. And, of course, even if he did find her at school, there wasn't much guarantee they'd get to talk.

There was a knock at the door.

'Come in!' yelled Mr Eddington, annoyed that the class was being interrupted.

Jules sat bolt upright. Walking into class was Theo.

He looked ridiculous. His Coat was doing a very poor impression of contemporary fashion, in fact, it started to change a little as Theo entered until Theo hissed at it to stop. So it stayed halfway towards looking a little better but still like nothing anyone would ever wear. His pants were wrong, his shoes were those trainers he tried once before that looked like trainers but with just too many bits of webbing and plastic bits and orange swoops and inserts. His hair was a moderate crimson but it was still louder and brighter than anyone else's in the room.

Mr Eddington stared at him.

The class stared at him.

Jules froze.

Theo smiled at everyone, and glanced at the blackboard. 'Hi ho!' he said. 'That's what you say, isn't it?' he asked, nodding towards Jules, who remained frozen. 'Algebra?' he continued, sneering at the board. 'Aren't you all a bit old? Is this the class for the moonheads?'

Mr Eddington recovered himself. 'Who are you? What do you want?'

'Ah, yip, or yay, as I think you say. Theodore Pine Four is the handle on the Code, sorry to interrupt the learning session, but the capital would like to speak to Jules Santorini.'

Theo beamed as though this was all very clever and as though he'd got it just right.

'The capital?' said Mr Eddington. 'What's the capital?'

Theo blinked, looking a bit flustered. 'The capital – it's you know, the guy where we went that time. The guy who runs things. You come in and say that and you can just go, yip?'

Mr Eddington's eyes narrowed. After fifteen years' teaching, he suspected everyone. 'Would you mean, the Principal?'

Theo thought about this for a moment. 'I might.'

'And why would the Principal want to see Jules Santorini, uuhh, what was your name again?'

'Theodore. Ahhh, he didn't say.'

'Really. I believe Ms Compton's usual practice is to send a note.' Mr Eddington stared at Theo.

Theo grinned and then stopped and tried to look serious. His hair went yellow for a moment until he got it under control. The class was silent, loving this.

Jules was feeling sick with nerves and astonished all at once. What was Theo doing back here?

'Santorini! Come up here. The rest of you, on with the set problems. I'll come around in a moment and answer any queries. I'll just deal with these two first.'

Jules got up, walked to the front of the class and stood next to Theo.

'Right,' said Mr Eddington. 'You know why clowns like you make me angry?'

'Nip. I can't say I do —'

Jules started a coughing fit. Theo got the message.

'You make me angry, because I don't want to spend any time dealing with idiots like you. I want to teach the class. I want the class to learn. I want to go home. Tiny-minded peaheads like you ruin my day.' Mr Eddington was at his most withering.

'Really?' said Theo. 'Then why do you have:

$a^2 + ab + b^2 = (a + b)^2$?

Surely it's 2ab. And then to do that, you don't have to do that . . .'

Mr Eddington was giving Theo his ice-man look, which had never been known to fail before. Students froze, knowing that they had sailed beyond the point of no return and they were now about to be entrapped by icebergs. Jules was having a coughing fit worthy of someone with tuberculosis and trying to contain Theo but Theo was noticing none of it. He was absorbed in the equations on the board.

'My clones, you Mil 3 people – you make Sparky the Wonder Neanderthal look like a genius. Ahhh, Screen, let's delete everything from 2c onwards, Oak Eye? Let y be the sum of 2 psi x . . . yip, that'll be better.'

Theo stood back. 'What's wrong with your screen? Nothing's happening.'

Mr Eddington was frozen himself. He'd never come across a student who could resist the ice-man look. But this strange boy was acting like nothing had happened, as though he, Simon Total Control Eddington, was smiling warmly upon him and encouraging his efforts.

Theo was now leaning forward and rubbing his finger on the board. 'It's not a screen!' Theo sniffed at the white dust on his finger. 'It's some kind of dust.'

'Technically, it's a form of calcite, $CaCO_3$, formed from the remains of fossilised marine shells,' Theo's Coat spoke up. 'Locally it's known as "chalk". Simple but effective communication technology for quite a few centuries.'

'Ah, Mil 3!' sighed Theo. 'Still just banging rocks together, aren't you? A little smarter than Sparky but not much!'

'YOU!' Mr Eddington unfroze and boiled over. 'GET OVER HERE.'

'Sip! Here I am,' said Theo, leaping across to stand next to Jules again. 'By the way, Jules, we gotta go.'

'RIGHT. I have had ENOUGH!' The autopilot was off, and Mr Eddington was flying dangerously low. His words were whipping around the classroom, lashing the boys. Jules was cowering but Theo didn't even seem to notice.

From inside his Coat, Theo brought out a JumpMan. It was a JumpMan Pro, and it hovered between them. From a pocket he drew out the familiar red remote.

'Oak Eye? We right?' he asked. 'Sorry about this, but need your boy. Bit of an emergency,' he apologised to Mr Eddington, who was now caught between a red-faced explosion and utter bewilderment.

Theo pressed the red button on the remote and they were gone.

JumpSite! Zine

Contents

ZONE ▸ JumpSite! Zine
ITEM ▸ 32654U-83-527840/JSZ346
VIEW ▸ Contents Page Edition #13

chapter five
Wrong Place, Wrong Time

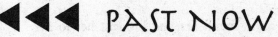 PAST NOW

LATE MORNING, TUESDAY ◀ EARLY MIL 1

Lavinia had been sitting quietly in the sun, thinking about how her life had changed over the last few days. She was home again but soon she would return to the villa in the country for good. As soon as she was married.

She'd always known the day would come. Lavinia understood that this was how it was always done and this is what her mother had done and her mother before her, and how important it all was. But she felt so sad that her childhood had ended so quickly.

A life of being her mother stretched out before her. She would be looking after a house, in charge of servants and slaves, making sure everything was ready each day, looking after the children —

Children!

She was going to have children?

She was only thirteen.

It wasn't until the feast, out at the villa, when her mother had talked about the dress, that it had all come thundering down on her.

At Fortunatus' villa, she'd run away from the banquet and hidden behind a pot of olives in a store room for two hours and cried.

Finally the slaves found her and brought her to her mother. She'd been made to stand and apologise to everyone for bringing shame and misery to such a happy occasion. What a selfish girl she was. How could she have anything but joy in her heart? It was such an honour to be marrying into such a family. Such a handsome husband with such wealth and prospects ... Her mother and her father had droned on and on and she'd tried hard to look as though she understood what they were saying and felt it in her heart of hearts.

And so she'd sat in the sun, henna baking dry on her hands, wishing she could just be a schoolgirl again. When a figure had suddenly appeared in the middle of the courtyard.

Instinctively she'd hidden behind a pillar. Who could this be? What kind of creature could just suddenly appear like that? Only a god perhaps. Or maybe a wood nymph. Perhaps an evil sprite, a demon or even an imp, or perhaps the witch who had been filling her with evil thoughts.

She'd been scared to peek out and look. If this was a god choosing to just suddenly appear in the middle of her house then she should be very careful. Make a god angry and you could spend the rest of your days as a hair louse. Or if it was not a god, but a nymph, then it might carry her off to take part in some kind of bizzare ritual near the top of the smoking mountain. She wasn't quite sure what sprites or imps might do, but she didn't want to tangle with one just in case. And if it was the witch, well, who knew what other kind of evil spells it might be willing to cast.

But now Lavinia had to look, just to see what the god, nymph or imp was up to now.

Something about this figure was distinctly ungodlike. In fact, apart from the strange clothing and even stranger language it was speaking, Lavinia thought it looked a lot like a girl her own age. A pleasant-looking girl wearing very peculiar garments and large bright orange things on her feet.

Whatever it was, it was wailing and moaning, and sounded very upset. 'Oh no. Oh No. Oh NOOOOO! Oh, this is really bad. Oh where am I? Quincy? QUINCY? Oh, this is not good. Not good. Not good!'

The creature looked wildly around the courtyard and caught sight of Lavinia. 'Hello!' it yelled. 'Don't be scared! You've got to help me! Where am I? What is this place, Oh God, I can't believe I'm asking this – what *YEAR* is it??'

Lavinia backed away. The strange creature was coming at her. It was talking loudly and making strange gestures. Up close she could see the peculiar texture of its clothes. It even smelt a bit strange. Where had it come from?

Lavinia looked around. Where had everyone gone? There was so much bustle as everyone got ready for the wedding, she couldn't believe that she was somehow alone with this apparition.

And it kept on trying to talk to her. 'Right. Right. Got to think,' it was saying. 'Quincy's made a mistake. I'm not back home. This is somewhere else. Maybe it's like a theme park or something. Hello? Is this DisneyWorld?

Do you speak English? Anyone else around? Oh God, Oh God, I'm in big trouble here.'

Even though the creature was babbling away, the language sounded kind of familiar.

Then something struck her – the creature was frightened. It was as scared as she was. And now it was smiling at her.

'Hi! What about French? *Ou suis moi?* That any good? *Ou moi je suis? Non? Qu'est ce que moi?* Not French. Well, that's it – although I can say hello in Indonesian, but somehow, I don't think that's going to help.'

The creature shrugged but kept smiling at Lavinia and then started to do something very odd. 'WHERE [shrug, scratch head], AM [large circling movement with hands] I? [clasp both hands to chest, shrug some more, hands held upwards]'

None of this meant anything to Lavinia. She took a step or two backwards and the creature dropped its hands by its side and let out a moan of frustration. 'Oooh. This is very very bad.'

It moved away from Lavinia to a window and took a look out into the street. It gasped audibly and its hand went to its mouth.

'Oh my God, this is really like ancient Rome or something. If this were DisneyWorld, I don't think it would stink this much.' The creature turned around, leant against the wall and slid down to the floor, then dropped its head in its hands and moaned some more. 'This is like what happened to Franklin. Or to Theo. This is not just a mistake. I've been sent somewhere. No one knows where. I don't have a JumpMan and I could be anywhere.' It started to cry softly to itself and hugged its knees.

Lavinia watched all this in astonishment. Gods don't cry. Neither do nymphs or imps. This was definitely a girl, crying and looking like she wanted to be somewhere else. Lavinia had been crying often in the last few days. She'd felt like crying just as the girl had turned up. When she did cry, she did exactly what this girl was doing right now. She curled up small and bawled her eyes out.

Lavinia moved a little closer. The girl was snuffling and wiping her nose. Lavinia felt a moment of daring. She went and sat down close to the girl.

The girl lifted her head and looked at her. She smiled through snot and tears and then laughed a little as she dried her eyes on the back of her sleeve. 'I don't suppose you've invented tissues yet, have you?' she said.

Lavinia smiled at her and the girl smiled back.

'Hello,' the girl said. 'Sorry to just drop in on you like this, but really, it wasn't my idea.'

Lavinia had no idea what the girl had just said, but she

smiled again and then spoke. 'Who are you? Is there something you want? Are you the daughter of Apollo? Or Zeus?'

'Woah!' It was the girl's turn to look surprised. 'You speak! But what are you saying? What language is that?'

Lavinia had no reply. She just smiled and nodded her head.

'OK,' said the girl. 'Let's start at the beginning.' She turned around and faced Lavinia then reached out and took Lavinia's hands in her own. Lavinia was startled to feel the warmth of the girl's hand, the softness of her skin. It was just like her own.

The girl put her hand flat on her own chest. 'Gen. Genevieve. Gen. Me. Gen. Gen.' She said it a few more times, pointing at herself. 'You say it?' she asked.

Lavinia thought for a moment. She wasn't quite sure what was meant, and she wasn't quite sure what the girl wanted her to do. But she thought it was a bit like a lesson with Claudius, so she'd just repeat what she had just heard.

'Gen,' she said. 'Gen.'

The girl looked surprised and pleased and nodded happily. 'Gen. That's right. Good. I'm Gen. And you?'

'Gen,' Lavinia said again.

Gen shook her head. 'No, that's me. What's your name?' She pointed at Lavinia.

Lavinia felt a bit confused. When she said Gen the first time, the girl had been very happy. Now she said it a second time and the girl was frowning and pointing at her. And then in a rush it came to her. Gen was the girl's name. She was asking Lavinia what her name was.

She smiled and mimicked Gen's gesture, putting her hand flat on her chest. 'Lavinia,' she said. 'Lavinia.' And then to show how much she understood, she put her hand on Gen's chest and said, 'Gen.'

Gen gave a little shout of triumph, 'Yes! Excellent! Now we're getting somewhere.'

Then Lavinia's mother came up the stairs. 'Lavinia! Where are you? By the gods, Lavinia, there's so much to do, this is not the time to play games.'

Gen withdrew into a dark corner behind a column. Lavinia stepped forward.

Her mother must have seen the guilty and worried look on Lavinia's face. 'What were you doing?' she asked, stopping and regarding Lavinia with a look of suspicion.

'Nothing. Just drying my hands and my hair, like you said.' Lavinia moved away from where Gen was hiding, out into the middle of the courtyard. She wasn't quite sure why she was protecting Gen but it seemed like the right thing to do.

'Well come along. They'll be done. Let's get dressed and go through what's going to happen.'

Lavinia's mother turned and walked away. Lavinia followed, trying to get a glimpse of her new friend. Gen caught her eye. They nodded to one another and then Lavinia disappeared around the corner.

Gen was left alone.

She slid down to sit on the stone floor behind the column.

She was somewhere in Rome or Greece or one of those places. The buildings, the clothes gave it away. Why had she trusted Quincy? He wasn't here and this was not Fifteen Billion and Seventy-three.

How would anyone find her? Only Jules might think she'd been TimeJumped somewhere, but he was in Mil 3. What could he do? It's not like he had a JumpMan under his bed. And there was no reason for Franklin or Theo to come looking for her. Franklin, she'd pretty much told never to visit her again, and as for Theo, he seemed too busy being famous. But even if they knew she was missing, how would anyone know she was here?

Wherever here was. She didn't even know where here was.

She felt incredibly scared and started to cry again.

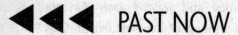

◀◀◀ PAST NOW

They blinked and they were elsewhere, elsewhen
and in every other sense a long way from home. Jules knew
immediately when he opened his eyes that they were not
just a few thousand years ago, or even a few thousand
kilometres away. They were millions of years back in time.
They were so far back, that if they'd been in orbit above the
Earth, the islands and the continents would have looked
different. Down on the ground, everything was different. The
air was full of smells he'd never smelt and it even seemed
to have a different texture from the air of Mil 3. The soil
seemed different. The clouds in the sky were odd shapes
and streaks. Jules and Theo were standing on a small
rounded hill. Behind them ran a dark purple mountain
range, jagged and threatening. It seemed new, like it had
been pushed up only a few days ago. Smoke curled from
the top of a peak, which was broken off like a volcano. Thick
forests covered the slopes, sliced by raging rivers with
cascading waterfalls that surged out of the range and across
the plain in front of them. The plain was covered in rich green
grass, somehow more vibrant than the greens of the bush

around Jules' city. Everything just seemed lusher – even the dirt in the gullies was richer and more chocolatey. Bugs the size of turtles and dragonflies like small birds scuttled and buzzed around them. Everything looked young and vital.

Perhaps the other clue that they were now millions of years in the past was the herd of stegosaurus passing in front of them.

Jules turned to Theo. 'Where?! What?! How did?! Why?! When?!' he spluttered.

'I think you left out Who?!' said Theo, grinning at Jules. 'Hip, Jules, it's me! Theo! Aren't you pleased to see me, Dodoboy?'

'Yes,' Jules got out eventually. 'But, but, but –' Jules was stuck, like an old CD.

'I know. It's a bit of a shock,' said Theo. 'Take your time. How's my hair looking? It was so hard to make it flat and dull like yours.'

Theo's hair was now a rich jet black with two broad yellow stripes up the middle.

Jules nodded. 'No, it looks fine.' He tried to ignore the nearby dinosaurs and focus on what the hell Theo was doing here in the first place.

'Theo, what the hell are you doing here?'

'Here?'

'Well, not here as such, yes here, but there, back in the classroom. Theo, what's going on?'

'Ahh, that'll take a bit of explaining,' said Theo. 'I better give you the short version. Over the weekend, Franklin comes to see me. He and my parents were old friends, so he sneaks in one night. Zip knows why he didn't drop in earlier. We start talking and, I don't know, ever since the whole pizza thing, I haven't felt right. I'm yesterday's ClickDown, that's for sure, but that's not it. We can't put it together, but the way Quincy just doesn't seem to care about Rule 1, and the way he seems so keen on changing stuff, it doesn't seem right.

'I mean it's been fun being famous and stuff, but it's been going on for too long. Someone's wanting me to be out there and it can only be Quincy.

'Anyway, Franklin gets me thinking and so I decide, just for a while, to go along with him. I'll keep a bit of an eye on Quincy and maybe just once in a while check that you two are Oak Eye.

'So, Franklin gives the co-ords, I Jump in this morning and get this – Gen's gone!'

'What? What do you mean?' Jules was shocked.

'Gone. Not there. She arrived at school, didn't go to class. Somewhere in there, between those annoying metal cupboards you have for making your clothes stink and keeping bits of old lunch in and the door of her first class, she disappeared.'

Jules shook his head, not really understanding. How

could she just disappear? He looked around. In front of them was a herd of maybe a thousand stegosaurus. Some were feeding, others were just ambling by. Every now and again one would raise its head from the grass and sniff the air or look about and then go back contendedly to munching. They looked like a docile herd of cows, except they were grey-green, as big as elephants, had strange bony plates coming out of their back and a tail that was equipped with some wicked-looking spikes. So not much like cows at all, really.

None of them had looked at the creatures watching them from the low hill. Seeing as how it would be about another 50 million years before there was anything walking around on two legs, as Jules and Theo were, perhaps they just didn't even register in their pea-sized brains.

'We're visible right?' asked Jules.

'Oh, yip. She needs to be able to see us even if we can't see her.'

'What?'

'She might be invisible. We don't know.'

'What are we doing here?'

'Here? I'm not quite sure. Franklin's given me some pre-sets to check out. I don't know what this one is.'

'No, I mean what are we doing?' asked Jules again. 'Why are we TimeJumping to look at dinosaurs? Shouldn't we be looking for Gen?"

'Oh, we are looking for Gen,' explained Theo.

'Here?' said Jules. 'Why would she be here?'

'Don't know,' replied Theo.

Jules felt like he and Theo had drifted off down different roads. He turned and grabbed Theo by the lapels of his Coat.

'Theo! Gen probably just went home again, or something like that. Why are we here? Or anywhere? Why aren't we looking for Gen?'

'Oh, I see,' said Theo. 'Franklin's pretty sure that Quincy has TimeJumped Gen.'

'Why?'

'He's not sure. But he probably wants to do it to you as well.'

'Why?'

'Don't know that either,' shrugged Theo. 'Franklin's just convinced that if I Jumped into Gen's bedroom with you there, then Quincy must have some interest in you two. He just can't figure out what that might be. No offence, Jules, but so far neither of you seem worth going to this much trouble for.'

Jules tried to turn the last comment into a positive. If he was worth getting rid of then he must be very special. Although it might be better to be not very special and then no one would want to get rid of him.

'TimeJumped Gen?' he asked after a while.

'Yip.'

'Where?'

'Ah, well, we don't know.'

Jules considered that for a moment. 'But Franklin thinks she might be here?'

'Ummm, probably not. But we kind of have to check everywhere.'

'Everywhere? Every JumpSite?'

'Yip, and everywhere else.'

'Everywhere else? You mean, everywhere in the last fifteen billion years?

'From the Big Bang till Yesterday, as TimeMaster likes to say. Franklin's trying to narrow it down.'

Jules gazed out hopelessly at the dinosaurs and the lush vegetation. Why would Gen be here?

~ *You putting this all together?* asked his brain.

~ *Gen's missing.*

~ *They don't know where.*

~ *She could be invisible.*

~ *And she could be anywhere in Time.*

~ *Anywhere.*

~ *Anywhen.*

'Franklin thinks that Quincy would have sent her somewhere significant,' Theo explained. 'But somewhere dangerous. So we're looking at those spots first.'

'Dangerous? Is this spot dangerous?'

'Must be somehow,' said Theo, looking at the calmly grazing stegosaurus and the gently waving grasses.

'Should we look around?'

Theo shrugged. 'Yip. Nip. Which way would we look?'

Jules felt even more hopeless. No sign of Gen.

~ *But she could be just over the hill.*

~ *Or just over the next hill.*

~ *Or not here at all.*

~ *Or here last year.*

~ *Or invisible.*

He turned to Theo. 'She could be anywhere, Theo. Anywhere. How do we even know we're looking in the right direction? What if we go now and she Jumps in as soon as we leave? She could be behind that tree. She could be invisible. How are we —'

But Theo wasn't listening to him. He was looking up at the sky. He was starting to shake his head.

'Oh, nip,' he said quietly. 'Moons of Mars, this is so unboid. This is exactly the kind of Now where Quincy would send her. Jump her here and five minutes later she's gone forever!'

Theo started to run, away from the herd of stegosaurus.

Jules jogged after him. 'What is it, Theo? What are you talking about?' he yelled.

Theo pointed up at the sky, where a large yellow ball

with a tail that reached halfway to the horizon was streaking towards land.

'That! That's the Asteroid that Kills the Dinosaurs. See? This is a Huge Site with the Extreme Jumpers. You Jump in here and set the JumpMan for automatic JumpBack the moment the asteroid hits. The thrill is to leave it as late as possible – just before the shock wave of the explosion hits you! If she's here and she can't Jump out of here . . .' Theo trailed off.

Jules looked over his shoulder. The stegosaurus, all contentedly munching away a few seconds ago, had started to trot. In their direction.

Theo started yelling. 'Gen! GEEEENNNNNNNN!'

Jules started panicking.

The horizon lit up. The sky ripped open and an intense white light stabbed through.

~ *Do you know the expression 'between a rock and a hard place'?*

~ *Brain, I'm not really interested right now.*

~ *You're between a herd of dinosaur and the asteroid that kills them. I'd be looking for a rock and a hard place myself right now.*

Jules kept on running. What else was there to do? He had to keep up with Theo. He had the JumpMan. If Gen was here, they were going have to run right into her in about the next three seconds or it wasn't going to matter.

Theo was screaming still, but Jules couldn't see the use. The noise of the dinosaurs was deafening. They were catching up. Their hooves were raising clouds of dust, and there was a faint roaring that seemed to be getting louder.

In all the confusion Jules lost Theo.

~ *Better find him. He's got the JumpMan.*

~ *I KNOW!*

Jules screamed, 'THEEEOOOOO!' It felt like he'd whispered in the dark. He breathed in a huge mouthful of dust at the same time that nearly choked him.

The ground was shaking now as the herd started to gallop. They seemed very close. Jules lost all sense of direction.

And then he was engulfed in a blinding light.

The asteroid had struck the Earth.

All became white, and the world went into negative. What was black was white. Jules could see, but it took a moment to figure out what he was seeing. That seething mass coming towards him must be the herd. And that tiny figure rooted to the spot was Theo.

Jules sprinted over to him.

He grabbed Theo by the arm, but Theo didn't move. He'd been staring at the light as it seared through them, and now his hair was standing upright, his eyelids were pinned back in his head, and his eyeballs were starting out of their sockets like a cartoon character.

Jules reached into the pocket of Theo's Coat. There was the remote.

He held onto Theo's arm, and as a huge roaring noise filled their ears like mud he hit the button. All went quiet.

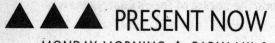
Jules felt feeling returning. His legs and arms tingled, as if they'd just suffered extreme pins and needles. His ears were ringing, as if they'd had car alarms installed, and his throat was dry and raw.

Theo's hair was stiff with dust and standing on end. His face appeared slightly sunburnt, as if it had been lightly fried in the light of the explosion. He slowly and deliberately blinked a few times and then started coughing in a rasping and painful way to try and clear his throat.

Jules looked up. Mr Eddington was staring at him.

Then he looked around at the class.

Everyone was very quiet. And very still.

Jules nudged Theo, who was coughing and hacking in a very unpleasant way.

'Wip? What's the deal?'

Theo caught sight of the utterly still, unblinking face of Mr Eddington. Then he too looked around at the very still, very quiet class. 'Wip! What happened to them?' he wheezed.

'I think it's what happened to us,' suggested Jules.

Theo looked at Jules, who was now white with dust

and dirt, and whose clothes had faded in the burst of white light. 'Do I look as bad as you?" asked Theo.

'A little worse. Your hair's not even trying.'

Theo put a hand up to touch his hair. He pulled it back in alarm. 'No colour?' he whispered hoarsely.

Jules shook his head sadly.

Mr Eddington straightened up a little.

The boys looked up at him.

Mr Eddington's mouth moved a few times and then he got it working. 'Principal. Go,' he managed.

Then he turned away from them and stared out at the rest of the class.

The class kept staring at Jules and Theo.

'I think we should go,' said Jules.

'Good idea, ' said Theo.

They started to back out of the classroom, watched by every student and studiously ignored by Mr Eddington.

'Class,' said Mr Eddington.

'Sir,' the class said in unison.

'Get on with your work,' he ordered.

'Yes, sir,' they replied, again in unison.

Mr Eddington sat down. The class opened their books and then stared at them. Mr Eddington sat staring at the grain of the wood in his desk. They remained like that for the next half hour, mutual shock slowing ebbing away to be replaced by mutual denial.

Jules and Theo had disappeared. Gone for a good part of the class. When they'd disappeared, Mr Eddington had just moved very slowly and carefully over to his desk and sat down. He'd said nothing. The class had said nothing. No one really knew what to do. A strange boy had come in; Jules Santorini had disappeared with him. Were they all dreaming? And then they'd both reappeared, but looking like they'd survived an earthquake or something.

It couldn't have happened. So it didn't happen.

Once out of the class, Theo and Jules walked quickly down the corridor and then started to run, relief at their escape flooding through them.

'Extreme!' whooped Theo. 'No one's ever left that Site so late!'

'Wimps!' yelled Jules. 'Mil 3 rules!'

They both laughed and fell against one another, wrestling to cover up the desire to hug. They separated and grew quiet, both thinking the same thing.

'Was Gen there, do you think?' Jules asked after a while.

Theo shrugged and shook his head.

'I don't know. If Franklin's right, then that's the kind of place Quincy would send someone he wants to get rid of. But I guess if she was there, we would have seen her.'

"Why?' yelled Jules, turning and grabbing Theo.

'We don't even know if she's visible? She could have been just over the hill. We're never going to find her. We could Jump to a different site every ten seconds and still never go to the one she's at at the precise time she's there!'

Theo shrugged. 'I know, I know. But what are we going to do? Not look?'

May as well, thought Jules. But he didn't say that. 'Well, I don't know,' he said instead. 'Are we going to Jump everywhere we can?'

'That's the plan so far, Jules. Let's go find Franklin. He should be out the front somewhere.'

But Franklin wasn't out the front. He was walking around the corner towards them. With Stevie Wan.

'Jules!' yelled Franklin.

'Franklin!' yelled Theo.

'Stevie,' said Jules weakly.

Stevie stopped and looked over his sunglasses. 'Do these guys play anything?'

'I don't think so . . .' said Jules.

'Pity.' Stevie nodded slightly at Jules. 'Later.'

Stevie walked off, and Jules gathered that the 'later' referred to the rehearsal he was meant to attend after school. What was it about this Monday, that everything had to happen at once?

'So Theo told you?' Franklin grabbed Jules by the arm.

'Yes, yes, he told me,' said Jules wriggling free. 'All we have to do is search the entire Universe, second by second, and we should be able to find her.'

'That's about right,' said Franklin. 'Except I do know Quincy. He wouldn't just send her anywhere. I mean, if I wanted to get rid of her – and I don't – but if I did, I'd just send her to some bubbling mud pond, two billion years ago, and that would be it! You don't last long when there's no oxygen in the atmosphere!' Franklin laughed at his own joke. 'But it's not me! Right?' He pushed his face into Jules. 'Don't be like Gen. Trust me! I might be weird, but I'm not trying to kill you.'

Again Jules pulled away. 'But why?' he half yelled. 'Why is Quincy trying to kill me?'

'I DON'T KNOW! Great helix, you're as bad as your girlfriend!' yelled Franklin. 'You want to wait until he Jumps you into the middle of World War Two or SHALL WE GO AND LOOK FOR GEN????'

Jules tried to calm Franklin down. 'OK, OK, I'll help, I'll help.'

'Rip,' said Franklin. 'I want to see those hideous girlfriends of hers. Maybe they saw something.'

The bell rang for the end of class. Jules led Franklin and Theo round to the corridor where the girls' lockers were.

Jules tried to ignore the constant stream of comments that Franklin and Theo attracted. In fact, the only ones who didn't have something to say were any of the students from Mr Eddington's class. They did the complete opposite – they pretended not to see them at all.

Then Kyeela, Sonja and Bonnie came up. They were all walking closely together and looked like they'd been crying.

'Jules!' said Bonnie. 'What are you doing here?'

'Where's Gen?' sobbed Sonja.

'What's going on with you two?' demanded Kyeela. 'And who's this – hang on, it's that kid, your cousin.'

'Hi ho, girls!' said Theo, brightening up a little. 'Let me see, Byeela, Conjac and Sonnie? And you thought I'd forget.'

The girls seemed impervious to Theo's charms and were now all staring at Franklin.

'We don't have a lot of time, Jules!' Franklin said.

'Right, right.' Jules wondered what to tell them. 'Umm. We might know where Gen's gone,' he began. 'But we need to know what happened, OK?'

'She just vanished!' blurted out Bonnie.

'She was walking along with us, and then she suddenly stopped,' said Kyeela.

'I turned around and she was talking to some fat guy. Dressed really weird,' added Sonja.

'Quincy!' exclaimed Theo.

'She listened to him, nodded a bit. And then –' Bonnie couldn't finish.

'They just went!' Sonja and Kyeela finished together.

Franklin pushed forward into the little group.

'You can help, girls. Jules, we can't do this here. Is there a room or somewhere we can go?'

Jules thought for a moment. Music rooms. No one was ever in the practice rooms, except for Marcia Morrison, who never did anything else.

'Come on,' he said, and they hurried off.

Marcia's scales greeted them as they entered. She was in the first room. They went to the end of the hall and crammed into a room full of clarinet cases and an upright piano.

'Right, girls,' began Jules. 'This might all be a bit hard to believe —'

Franklin stepped forward, cutting Jules off. 'No time!'

He pointed a remote at the three girls. He and the girls vanished.

Thirty seconds later they came back. Franklin looked harassed; the girls were white with fright.

Jules and Theo grinned at them. 'What did you see?' asked Jules.

'It's called TimeJumping, girls,' said Theo. 'Good fun, once you get used to it.'

None of the girls could speak.

Franklin clapped his hands in front of their faces.

'Right, you three. Girls, girls girls! Gen's your friend, you want to help her?'

They started to focus a little on Franklin.

'Try and concentrate, girls. We don't have much time. For reasons that we won't worry about right now, the most powerful man in the world of Fifteen Billion and Seventy-three wants her out of the way. What you just did was a TimeJump.'

The girls looked as though Franklin might have been discussing some of the more intricate details of camel anatomy.

Franklin continued anyway. 'It was nice, wasn't it? That's the Princess Wedding JumpSite. It's the wedding of Princess Anna Magdálena of Portugal to Prince Roland of Ruritania. It's a beautiful story. The prince had searched for seven years and seven days for a bride and finally one rainy night – anyway, we've got no time for that now!'

Franklin remembered what they were meant to be doing. He dug into a bag slung around his neck and pulled out three JumpMans like the one attached to his arm. 'These are called JumpMans. They are my own design, and they're much better than the grapefruit Theo's using. Yours are already loaded with pre-sets. You press that button, you go to a site. You look around. You press the button again, you come back, report to me. Don't stay too long – just look around where you land. If she's there and she's visible, she'll probably be the centre of attention. Don't rescue her. Just come back and get me. You think you can handle it?'

The girls hadn't moved or spoken, and looked as though Franklin had been talking about camels in Urdu. Like Jules and Gen when they first encountered Theo, their minds were rejecting everything they were seeing and hearing. They were full of questions but they had no idea how to ask them.

'Fine!' said Franklin, checking the JumpMans then handing one to each girl. He showed them how to wear it. Franklin's model of JumpMan fitted itself onto each girl's arm, adjusting itself to be a tight but comfortable fit. There were no buckles or straps, and the girls were now peering at them closely.

'Oak Eye, you ready? Press the button!'

None of them did.

'Oh, Flip me out,' said Franklin, and he reached over and grabbed Bonnie's and pressed it for her.

'Krakatoa!' he said to Bonnie. 'Press it again to come back!'

'Inca Sacrifice!' he barked at Kyeela, who was looking wide-eyed and horrified as Bonnie disappeared. 'Don't forget. Press it again and you'll come back.'

'Hawaiian War Canoe!' he smiled at Sonja.

'I'll do it!' she said.

'Good!' said Franklin like a pleased teacher. 'See you soon!'

He turned to the boys. 'You ready?'

'Where are we going?' asked Jules.

'Nothing really dangerous. But I do want you two to go together. I've loaded a list on Theo's JumpMan. I'll be coming and going a bit myself, but if you need me, I should be here soon enough. Bye bye!'

Franklin waved cheerily as they pressed the buttons on their JumpMans.

Jules just had time to hear his brain asking,

~ *If the girls are going to like, Krakatoa, does that mean we're going somewhere much worse?*

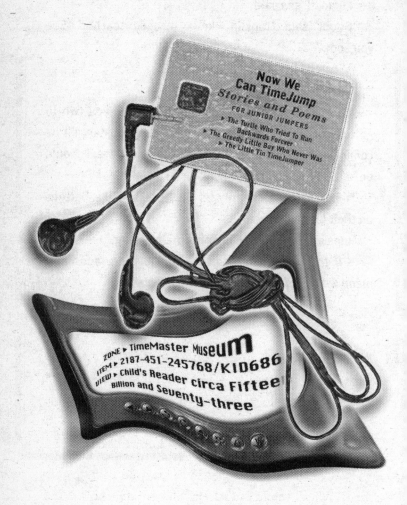

Now We
Can TimeJump
Stories and Poems
FOR JUNIOR JUMPERS

▶ The Turtle Who Tried To Run
   Backwards Forever
▶ The Greedy Little Boy Who Never Was
▶ The Little Tin TimeJumper

ZONE ▶ TimeMaster Mᴜsᴇᴜm
ITEM ▶ 2187-451-245768/KID686
VIEW ▶ Child's Reader circa Fiftee
Billion and Seventy-three

chapter six

No Time
to Lose

 PAST NOW
MIDDAY, TUESDAY ◀ EARLY MIL 1

Gen needed a plan. She needed a plan, because otherwise she would just sit behind this column and cry. She was thirsty and hungry. How was she going to get food? Where would she sleep? Should she stay in the house? Should she leave? Where would she go, if she did?

But one question overwhelmed the others. Where was she?

It seemed important to try and figure this out. Only when she knew where she was could she make some kind of plan. Without knowing where she was and when she was, she felt completely lost.

Ancient Rome, she decided. I'm in ancient Rome, or somewhere in Roman times.

Why? she immediately asked herself. Could be Greece, couldn't it? Or somewhere I've never even heard of. It could be ancient Persia or ... or ... Gen's list of ancient civilisations ran out at Persia. She knew there were a few more, but she didn't really know what they looked like or what they were called. Rome, she knew. It had buildings, and togas and sandals and there were gladiators. There'd been that movie where they had to go and fight lions or tigers or each other. Until one of them was dead. Great entertainment, she thought. Makes football look kind of tame.

Her mind was racing. What time was it? She even laughed at that. Do they have clocks? Was it afternoon or morning? She was actually losing track of time, which was another joke. She felt completely at the mercy of time. Time had dumped her here. Time would reveal what was meant to happen to her.

From behind the column, she'd noticed people coming

and going. There was something happening. And that girl, Lavinia, she looked like she'd been dressed up for something.

Clothes, Gen decided. I need clothes. At the moment, she was wearing jeans, trainers, a shirt and a jacket that had looked great that morning in Mil 3, but were totally out of place here in wherever she was. She looked like a visitor from another planet and another time.

That's exactly what I am, thought Gen. As she was about to succumb to another bout of tears, Lavinia stepped back into the courtyard and looked carefully around.

Gen whistled softly.

Lavinia smiled and ran over to her.

'Hi!' said Gen.

Lavinia said, 'Salve!' or something like that.

'Clothes,' said Gen, and she took off her jacket, screwing up her face. 'No good. Everyone stare and laugh.' Gen mimed all the actions and this time Lavinia seemed to understand what was needed.

She nodded and ran off.

A few minutes later Lavinia returned carrying a simple tunic and some sandals, like the people walking through the courtyard had been wearing.

Gen quickly put them on. Lavinia smiled. Now Gen looked like any other girl from her own time.

Gen looked down at the rough cloth tunic and the sandals and suddenly felt cold. Taking off her own clothes and putting on these felt like taking a step further into this world. She couldn't help wondering if she was ever going to need her clothes from Mil 3 again.

She rolled up her jeans, jacket and trainers, pointed to them and shrugged. 'I want to put these somewhere,' she said.

Lavinia seemed to be grasping everything Gen said very quickly now. She gestured, and they set off across the courtyard then through a door and down a corridor.

Lavinia pulled aside a curtain and Gen looked inside. It was more like an alcove than a room. There was a small, narrow bed with a thin blanket and tiny pillow, a slim cupboard, a jug of water and nothing else.

Lavinia took Gen's clothes and put them under the little bed. Then she smiled and nodded at her. They turned around to go.

'Lavinia!' The same woman, Lavinia's mother, was standing in the doorway. 'Will you not wander off? I can't believe you. You are getting married! You're acting like it's happening to someone else.'

Gen didn't understand a word, of course, but as the woman was talking, Gen noticed that her gaze started to drift to Gen's face. She frowned, issued a command and pointed down the corridor, before turning and walking briskly away. Lavinia followed, then turned to look at Gen. Smiling, she pointed in the same direction her mother had pointed.

Gen couldn't see many other options but to go where she'd been ordered, down the corridor and around a corner towards a doorway at the end.

As she approached she could hear clattering and lots of angry yelling. She could also smell food. Gen tiptoed cautiously towards the door and peered through.

It was a door to the kitchen. A dozen men and women were at work, scaling fish, cutting up meat, preparing vegetables. Hot bread was being pulled out of a raging oven.

Standing at a huge marble table in the centre was one of the burliest men Gen had ever seen. Big thick neck, great hams of arms, fingers like bananas. He was obviously the cook and definitely in charge. He was shouting at everyone and threatening them with an enormous cleaver. Occasionally he would clout someone with a spoon or stick of celery or anything that he could grab. As dishes were finished, they were presented to him for approval. He'd sniff them, stick a fat finger in the middle and then suck the sauce off a filthy nail. Then he'd grunt more orders or nod grumpily if the dish was ready.

For a long time Gen watched, fascinated. Then the cook caught sight of her. He pointed and yelled.

Gen froze. She should have run, but it seemed too late, and she could hear people coming down the corridor behind her.

The cook yelled again, turning purple. Gen didn't feel like she had much choice but to obey. The others looked up from their work, and she felt as though less attention would be better than more. So she straightened up and walked through the door and towards the marble table.

The cook pointed at a large silver platter.

Gen wondered what he wanted. She stood helplessly for a moment.

The cook yelled himself a deeper shade of purple, before picking up the platter and banging it on her head.

It hurt, and small tears started in her eyes.

Clearly the platter was meant to stay on her head, however, because the cook pulled up Gen's hands to grab either side of it.

Slaves or servants or cooks – Gen couldn't really tell – started to load her platter up with something until it became very heavy.

In front of her, two other slaves had loaded platters on their head.

The cook barked an order and the two slaves went out the door, balancing carefully. Gen followed. They went back through the door and across the courtyard, then into the house.

The rooms here were a blaze of light. Candles and torches burnt everywhere. Rich, colourful paintings of food, people dancing, beautiful women and strange creatures were on every wall. One room was crammed with people and they were all laughing and drinking from gold goblets.

Gen and the slaves entered, and Gen realised that the food on her head was nibblies to go with the drinks.

She started to move through the crowd. What was she now, a slave in a rich Roman house? What was going on, a party?

Then she saw Lavinia, seated on a silver throne at one end of the room beside a young man. They were holding hands and Gen could see that everyone seemed to be referring to them. This wasn't just a party, it was a wedding! Lavinia was dressed up because she was getting married! There were serving girls standing around her and off to one side was the woman she'd seen, who Gen presumed was Lavinia's mother. She was standing with a short man who was probably Lavinia's father.

Lavinia caught sight of Gen beneath the platter and stared at her. Gen pushed through the crowd towards her.

Suddenly the strangest thing happened. It was as though the floor buckled in slow motion. Suddenly Gen felt as if she was standing on sea rather than land. Her legs wobbled and went weak as the floor continued to shake and vibrate. There was a deafening noise and around her she saw other people lose their balance and start toppling into one another. Women were screaming, and men were falling on top of them as they tried to help. From the ceiling chunks of stone and masonry fell down with an enormous crash of dust and plaster. A great crack split one of the walls and columns suddenly seemed to be made of cheap plasticine, not stone and marble.

Gen felt seasick and the platter she was carrying crashed to the floor. Food was scattered everywhere and two dogs that had yelped and hidden when the calamity started now darted forward and began scoffing down the meats and the small cooked birds.

Earthquake? wondered Gen as she picked herself up. Around her people were checking that their limbs were still there and still worked. Then they all headed for the doors.

Lavinia ran forward and grabbed Gen's arm and they joined the crowd.

Outside there was a great clatter and yelling. People were in the streets examining their houses, staring at the cracks that had opened up in the roadway and shouting excitedly to one another. Lavinia and Gen huddled by a wall.

Now something was nagging at the back of Gen's memory. Something she'd done in school at some point. She couldn't quite make the connection but there was something about the street that looked familiar. Had she seen a picture of it in a book?

Gen turned to Lavinia. 'Where are we?' she asked.

Over the way part of the front of a building had collapsed. A fire had started down the street. The sky above them had become a swirling mix of intense light and dark, as if a huge thunderstorm was brewing.

Gen waved an arm around to indicate the whole city. 'Where am I? What's this place called?' She shrugged, rolled her eyes, did everything she could to try and communicate the question to Lavinia.

Lavinia watched her and nodded. 'Pompee,' Gen thought she said.

'Pompee?' Gen tried.

Lavinia nodded and smiled. 'Pompee!' she said again.

In Gen's mind, the connection fused. The earthquake, the strange light, the style of the buildings. She was in ancient Rome, all right. But not in Rome. She was in the pleasant seaside town of Pompeii. And now that she was outside she could see the mountain that dominated the town. At its peak smoke was curling into the sky. Gen was pretty sure the name of the mountain was Mount Vesuvius. And it was about to demonstrate most forcibly to the residents of Pompeii that it could do more than smoke a little. The long dormant volcano was about to become active again.

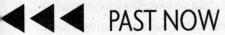
Jules' eyes opened wide. He and Theo were standing in a long low hall of some kind with high narrow windows of thick glass covered by wooden shutters. At the opposite end of the hall were solid-looking wooden doors, which had just been thrown open.

Five or six men marched in. 'Good morrow! We saw not your coach nor horse,' said one.

'Did you place them straight at stable?' asked another.

'Well, you are here now and mightily glad are we to see you.'

The men stepped forward and started shaking Jules' and Theo's hands and introducing themselves. 'Councillor Tom Alderley, and this is Squire Brookson. We've hired a notary from the next town, Master Addison, just back from the new university.'

Jules was stunned and hung back.

But Theo leapt in and was vigorously shaking hands. 'Good morrow!' he cried to each one. 'Hey ho, and hi derry derry!'

Theo seemed to know where they were. Jules thought for certain they were about to get into all sorts of trouble with these men, who seemed old and serious. They were wearing dark tunics, leather aprons, tights, simple leather shoes, thick coats and floppy hats. Everything was woven from wool or made of rough linen, and there was little decoration of any kind beyond a brooch to keep a cloak in place or a lumpy belt buckle. Jules was sure he glimpsed a knife in a leather holder on one man's belt and that was certainly a sword Squire Brookson had strapped to his side.

Jules was still in Mil 3 gear and Theo was in his usual extraordinary garb. Theo's hair was also changing colour as he happily greeted each of these men, from a kind of iridescent orange to a more neutral wheat colour. Jules was certain their appearance would give them away but the men made no comment about their outfits.

The introductions finished, the man who'd been doing most of the talking, Councillor Alderley, smiled grimly at them, and said, 'Strange times indeed. That they should send such young men abroad to hunt witches and devils. Strange, most strange.' The councillor looked at them closely and seemed about to challenge Jules, but then he thought again.

Jules had noticed that all of the men were quite short. They seemed nuggety and barrel-shaped, a bit like the dwarves in Snow White.

The councillor nodded, as though confirming something in his own mind. Then he clapped both Jules and Theo on the shoulders and led them towards a long table at the front of the hall. 'Here I think is where we shall conduct proceedings. I've seen it done in Norwich Town and we'll do it as was done there. You two shall sit here, we shall flank you. The accused shall be brought here in front of you. The usual tools and encouragements will be over there. Court sits at midday. Until then, please visit my inn, where good viands and good drink are yours, honoured sirs.'

The men bowed low and left, and the doors closed behind them with an ominous thud.

Theo turned and grabbed Jules, eyes wide with terror. 'Do you realise where we are?'

Jules shook his head.

'This is the Witch Burning. It's a Banned Site. Fifteenth century England. It's absolutely horrible. And they think we're the judges, here to decide if, if, if she should burn!'

'Well, let's just go then.' Jules reached for the remote.

Theo pulled it away. 'What if it's Gen?'

'What if who is Gen?'

'The accused. The one they are going to bring in at midday.' Theo waited for this to sink in. 'This is when they burn someone just because she has a black cat or can treat indigestion. If a girl dressed like Gen, talking like Gen, suddenly appears in the middle of a tiny, stinking, pig-ignorant, superstitious village like this one in the middle of Mil 2 do you think they would all gather round and want to chat? No, they'd want to barbecue her. They fry her, they feel safe! They *like* burning people!'

Jules got the point. 'So we have to wait? What if it's not Gen?'

Theo shrugged. 'We go.'

'So what do we do now?'

'Let's go have a look around. Maybe we can find her, and get out of here early.'

Jules just shook his head. He felt hopeless. A dull weight filled his stomach and his head felt all black.

~ Hey, could you get a bit positive? requested his brain.

~ Positive? Positive?? What's it matter if I'm positive? I can be as perky as a pixie, it's not going to help us find Gen.

~ Yes it is.

~ Brain – you're a brain. Could you act like one for once? What does it matter if I'm feeling good? Gen is somewhere in the last fifteen billion years. Me being cheerful is not going to help find her.

~ The answer is always in the present.

~ Oh, go and be a bumper sticker will you? Or one of those little books full of sayings that make ideal Christmas gifts that no one knows what to do with.

~ Oh, it's easy to sneer. But believe me, you start feeling hopeful, you'll think better. And you might come up with an idea for where she is.

I want to feel some hope, thought Jules.

~ *There you go. That's better already.*

~ *Shut up.*

They pushed open the doors of the hall and stepped outside. They were in a village of low rude huts thrown up around a well. Everything was filthy. There was mud everywhere. Dogs rolled in it. Sad, slow peasants hauled rough carts of grain through it. Others slogged across the quagmire carrying a hoe or a stick on their way to the fields. There were a couple of shivering trees. A donkey standing around looking thin and defeated. Women, some holding babies, were sloshing water into buckets. Children ran around them, fighting over bits of rotting vegetable. One girl sat firmly in the mud playing dolls with two mouldy pieces of what might have been potato.

A slight stench of sodden decay was coming off everything. The air was thick with smoke from cooking fires and it stung their eyes. Jules wondered if it ever really dried out here, and if anyone ever really got clean.

As Jules and Theo slopped out into the open, all activity stopped. Everyone turned and stared at them. And then just as quickly everyone started to disperse. The women picked up their buckets, nodded to one another and then scuttled back to their huts. Two men walking by offered an awkward nod in their direction and then tucked their heads down, quickened their walk and disappeared as soon as they could.

Even the dogs, chewing at their mangy backs, seemed to realise that something was wrong and skulked off to hide in some soggy bushes. The donkey seemed to be avoiding looking at them.

'This feels good,' said Theo.

'It's nice here,' said Jules. 'No wonder it's banned.'

'Yeah, you can only come here on May Day. Lot of dancing, and cider,' said Theo. 'Otherwise, yip, it's a bit bleak, isn't it? And don't they seem to love us!'

At the other end of the muddy square was a building a little larger than the ugly huts slouching around the square. Deciding that it must be the inn, Jules and Theo slopped their way over to it, looked at one another, shrugged, and decided to go in.

They pushed open the door and entered a low room with a fire in one corner and some benches and tables scattered around. Four old men bent over clay pots in one corner looked up at them briefly and then huddled back together, murmuring and occasionally jerking a thumb in their direction.

A short fat woman with no teeth waddled over to greet them. 'Keep your horse where you will, I'm sure you'll find much to warm you here.'

Jules had no idea what she meant but he smiled and nodded.

'You'll be wanting pottage? Comes with beer,' she said.

Theo nodded eagerly. 'Good cheer, good woman is good whatwithal and nonesuch as good cheer as may be had as is your good cheer, what ho!'

The woman turned back to regard Theo strangely. She looked at him for a little too long, long enough for most people to get uncomfortable under such scrutiny. Theo, however, smiled and posed for her.

Jules pulled him over to a table. 'I'd talk a little more simply, and I'd stop drawing attention to myself,' he suggested.

'Sorry,' said Theo. 'But I am blending in here, and speaking the language as they speak it. When in Ruritania do as the Ruritanians do.'

'It's Romans. Do as the Romans do,' corrected Jules.

'What would the Romans be doing in Ruritania?'

Jules gave up.

The food arrived. It was hot, and smelt like heated-up old socks.

There was no cutlery. Jules took a sip, scalded his tongue then wondered what the slippery thing was that slopped down his throat. He took a slurp of his beer. It was luke-warm and flat.

Theo fished around in the bowl and brought out a stringy piece of grey meat. 'What do you think this was?' he asked in a whisper that all seemed to hear.

Even though the four old men in the corner were studiously avoiding them, it seemed to Jules that he and Theo were the only thing they were concentrating on. The short, fat woman was also never far away, constantly circling their table with a broom of sticks, or wiping down their table with a rag that left a smear dirtier than anything there before. A boy with wonky eyes came in and lurked in a corner, pretending to look busy. Even the cats snoozing on the window sills seemed to sense that there was something going on, and opened one eye to stare at them.

'We have to eat it,' said Theo.

'I'll be sick everywhere,' said Jules.

'If you do that, they'll burn us too,' suggested Theo.

Ten minutes later the pair of them left the inn, slopped back across to the main hall, went around the back and threw up.

Then they went inside. They'd seen the village. Wherever the girl was being kept it wasn't out in the open, and so short of poking about in everyone's hut, there was nothing they could do but wait.

A few minutes later the doors were pushed open by two large burly men carrying a strange-looking table with metal clasps and a cog at one end. They set the table down then left, but were back soon after, carrying all kinds of odd objects, including a cage and a metal bucket full of hot coals. Into this they placed tongs, hot pokers and spikes. On the table they laid out hammers, more spikes and a range of other strange-looking devices, none of which you would let children play with. All of them had far too many sharp points, barbed bits and razor edges.

Jules and Theo had gone pale.

'That's – they're going to . . .' stuttered Jules.

Theo nodded and walked around the table and the implements. 'Yes, hot spikes to burn her, all kinds of manacles and blades to cut her. And this is what they fondly call the Rack.' Theo pointed to the table.

'The Rack?' said Jules, feeling faint.

'The Rack,' said Theo. 'Place Witch upon rack and then wind to stretch her.'

Jules felt sick again. Was Quincy this cruel? Would he send Gen to be tortured? And if he would, above all, why?

The doors of the hall were flung open once more. The men they had met earlier marched back in.

'Good morrow once more! I see the tools are here. We'll soon know if this little harlot's in league with Beelzebub!' Councillor Tom Alderley seemed far too enthusiastic about the whole process.

Theo stepped forward. 'My Lords!'

The men seemed a little surprised at being addressed thus but they gave Theo their attention.

'Let us confer if we may be so bold as to local custom. In some villages hey nonney nonney and nonesuch as may be told, a witch may be unstitched if she answer true. Be this and with a falalala as you like it hereabouts, be this such a place?'

Theo felt rather proud of this question and he stood grandly waiting for their answer.

Councillor Tom leaned forward, looking puzzled. 'I'm sorry, Great Priest of the Council, but I'm not sure I understood your question.'

Theo tried again. 'Be not I a ninnypot that I may not ask plain. If a witch saith "I am a witch", dost thou believe her?'

Tom's eyes narrowed a little. 'She may say she is a witch, but how will we know she is a witch unless the hot iron is placed upon the soles of her feet?'

'But if she says she is a witch, then we don't need the hot iron,' tried Theo, thankfully forgetting to speak the local lingo.

'Not need the hot iron?' The locals looked puzzled.

The talk of hot irons and the recent strange meal with beer was making Jules feel a little queasy.

Theo seemed strong, however. 'My Lords of . . . of . . .

hereabouts,' he continued. 'I tell you in Londinium, they use more modern methods.'

'Modern methods, Great Priest?'

'There, my Lords, many these days can tell a witch by counting the pimples on her nose. And all they do on these coals is toast crumpets!'

Councillor Tom looked even more puzzled. 'Crumpets?'

'A delicacy from the East!'

Now Jules felt more than a little queasy. He was frightened. These men weren't buying Theo for one second.

Councillor Tom shook his head and the other men looked similiarly displeased with Theo's talk of modern methods.

'Well, I don't quite follow the thinking there,' said Councillor Tom. 'She might confess to being a witch straight away to avoid the torture.'

The others nodded and murmured in agreement.

'Surely the clearest way to tell if she is a witch is to take this metal spike here and hold it fast against her naked flesh. If it truly burns her and burns her deep, then she is not a witch. For if she be a witch then surely she would use some spell to protect her from the hideous searing pain of a hot iron on the bare sole of the foot. Although, sometimes we have noted in the past, the truly evil witches allow themselves to be burnt in order to fool us into thinking they are innocent. So then we have no recourse but to use everything at our disposal.' Councillor Tom indicated the assembled implements of torture as though he was a shopkeeper showing off some new lines.

Jules covered his mouth and leaned back on the table.

'We are talking about rooting out the devil, are we not?' Councillor Tom continued. 'I do not grasp the weed by the head and tug. I dig deep and slash at the roots, so that the weed shall not spread and contaminate us all!' He finished off with great vigour and righteousness.

His companions murmured approval.

Theo opened his mouth to speak, but Councillor Tom still held the floor. 'No, I think it best, Great Priest, that we do it our way first and then maybe you can try your new methods from the city!'

The doors at the end of the hall were suddenly flung open.

The two burly men, dressed now in dirty black clothes, were dragging in a young girl. She was Gen's height, and seemed to be Gen's age. She was only barely conscious. Her head rolled forward and Jules couldn't see her face.

Both Jules and Theo rushed forward to help her but found themselves restrained by the councillor and the squire. The squire had half-drawn his sword.

Councillor Tom turned to them, a thin smile on his face. 'Let us see you now try one of your own kind!'

Jules and Theo looked at him, startled.

'I sent word two days ago that we had a witch, and we needed a trial with a priest. A priest would take a week at least to get here. Only a fellow witch could have got here so fast. And only a fellow witch would argue against the true methods of finding a witch.'

Councillor Tom drew in close, his knife now out and twitching in his hand. The others circled them to cut off any escape.

'But me thinks there is a way to settle this,' suggested Councillor Tom slyly. 'Try the girl! Try the girl, find her guilty, and we can think again upon your predicament!'

Jules looked at the girl lying face down on the floor. She was making no sound. It could be Gen.

No one spoke. Everyone was looking at Jules and Theo.

Jules looked at Theo and nodded. Not much choice right now but to go along with them.

'Umm, would you mind . . .' began Jules, and then realised that politeness was not really called for. 'Get up!' he tried again. 'Or rather, arise, ahh, wench, so that we may gaze upon your face and know if we are in the presence of a servant of Satan!'

~ *Not bad. Those heavy metal albums have come in handy.*

~ *Shut up! I really need to focus here.*

~ *Hey. I'm doing a lot of work behind the scenes, believe me.*

The girl got up slowly.

It wasn't Gen.

Jules looked at Theo. Theo stepped forward, unable to contain himself.

He drew Jules in close to him and together they stood over the girl. The Squire's sword was out, and the others were reaching for their knives.

Theo muttered into his collar. 'Coat I need full Voice Projection and let's go to Maximum Extend, Deep Black and High Collar, thank you.'

Theo's Coat turned as black as pitch. His collar stood up encircling his head. And he began to rise, as the Coat raised him up, until he was three metres tall and towering over everyone. 'Feeble people! Leave this place!' thundered Theo out of his Coat. He sounded like a deranged Shakespearean actor. 'Leave, or my master will seek your souls and suck them from you like a dog sucks a bone. What hope do you have against our power?'

The men drew back a little.

Theo pressed his advantage. 'Get ready Jules, we're going to Jump her with us,' he whispered. Out loud he said, 'This one is no mere witch! No concoctor of potions and spells. No rider of brooms black against the moon!

No wart ridder, gout tickler or crow keeper!'

Jules was amazed at Theo's language. Where was he getting all this stuff?

'This one has supped with the Devil and used no long spoon. She has danced to his tune and, in short, she is his paramour!'

Jules wasn't quite sure what a paramour was, but it had the desired effect on the men. They gasped in shock and the Squire's sword clattered to the ground. Master Addison, the notary, ran for the door, while the others grabbed at one another for protection.

'Wouldst we stay and menace you for daring to presume you could trifle with the likes of us. But He calls and we must go forth. We will darken your hearths no more, unless —' Theo paused and nodded, pleased with the next bit.

'The halls of our brimstone-laced palaces hear talk of you burning and torturing our kind. Do it but just once, and it will be your last act above the ground!'

Then Theo screamed. 'Now Jules!'

Jules grabbed the girl by the arm and leapt towards Theo.

Theo's Coat dropped back to their level. Theo grabbed Jules and the girl, and pressed the GoButton on the JumpMan.

There was an incredible clanging noise as the three of them materialised on the keyboard of a piano in the music room.

Perhaps most surprised was Stevie Wan, who was working on a new lyric. He often avoided things he didn't like, such as woodwork, by hanging out in the music rooms. He might write a song, or figure out a particularly choice riff or two.

'Stevie!' said Jules. 'Hi. Sorry, we'll get out of your way.'

Jules and Theo jumped down off the piano and ran for the door, dragging the girl with them.

'See you tonight!' called Jules, as they scurried outside.

Stevie watched them go. He didn't have any choice really. He was in deep shock and had temporarily lost the use of his limbs and his mind.

The school grounds were filling up. It was lunch time. Jules was totally disoriented by the sudden return to normality. It seemed almost more unreal than the witch burning trial they'd just left.

The girl between them whimpered and dropped to the ground, huddled over in a tight heap.

'What are we going to do with her?' asked Jules.

'I don't know!' said Theo. 'Should we have left her to be treated like toast?'

Jules shuddered. Such a horrible place and time. He bent down to the girl on the ground. 'Hi. Ummm, I'm Jules. Jules Santorini. Look, we aren't going to hurt you.'

The girl whimpered and drew in even more tightly.

'I'll see if I can find Franklin,' said Theo. 'You wait with her.'

Great, thought Jules. The entire school is starting to walk by, and I'm sitting here with a whimpering bag of rags. He bent over her again.

'Look, we want to help you. We saved you. Believe me. We came there to save you, to protect you. You're safe now!'

The girl stopped whimpering for a moment. She had her arms over her head for protection, but she turned her face just enough to scrutinise Jules out of one eye. 'But you're the Devil. You're demons and warlocks. You've flown me to hell! You're taking me to see Lucifer.' Her voice was rising and she was starting to scream very loudly.

'No, no,' said Jules. 'We're not the devil or anything like that. We just said that to get you out of there. We're just kids. We're just normal. Well, Theo's not, but I am.'

She calmed down a little. 'Where am I?' she asked very quietly.

'Oooh, that's a long story,' said Jules shaking his head slowly. 'I might get my friend Franklin to explain some of that to you.'

Theo ran up. 'He's out the front. Trying to blend in.'

Jules gently coaxed the girl up. 'What's your name?' he asked.

'Sarah,' she replied.

'Sarah. OK, I'm Jules. That's Theo. You're at a school. If you don't make eye contact with anyone, they tend to leave you alone. Took me two weeks to figure that out. Come on.' They walked off towards the front of the school.

Sarah tried to keep her head down, but there must have been too many wonders flashing by. She kept pointing at the buildings, she seemed overwhelmed by the sheer numbers of kids walking by, and when they got out the front, she hid herself against Jules' chest as the cars roared up and down the road outside.

'Franklin!'

Franklin climbed out of the shrubs in the front of the garden. 'The gardener is insane. I've never seen anyone so protective of a few plants. He keeps chasing me out of here. But if I stand on the street, that old guy with the Stop/Go sign keeps wanting to know what I'm doing. Who's this?'

Jules explained.

Franklin looked at them, horrified. 'You can't just Jump

people out! That's the whole point. That's what Quincy wants to do. You don't decide just to save someone.'

'But they were going to burn her, Franklin! Stick hot pins into her and then throw her on a fire. Look at her – she's the same age as us!'

'What do you want to do, go and rescue the thousands of people who were burnt as witches? Some of them were younger than her, you know. Do you want to rescue everyone who was tortured? Or everyone in prison? Or just the ones you happen to meet?'

'No! I don't know,' said Jules. 'But we couldn't leave her.'

Franklin nodded, letting some air out, and sat on the fence. 'Yip, I know, I know,' he said. 'There'd be something wrong with you if you could. But you know what? Think about this – things are better for her – but what about for everyone back in the village? You just appeared out of nowhere, and then disappeared again, taking a "witch" with you. They've never had such convincing evidence of the existence of witches and devils. What do you think is going to happen now, back there in that muddy, vulgar village you've just zapped out of? Hmm?'

A strange, cold feeling crept through Jules. He imagined Councillor Tom and shuddered.

Franklin made a consoling gesture. 'Don't worry too much about it,' he said. 'That whole period, really nasty.

But you get the point? That is the past. It is what happened, not what should have happened according to you.'

Franklin looked philosophical for a moment. His voice lost its usual hysterical edge. 'We do what we do and then we do the next thing. We are all the result of millions of years of tiny, minute-by-minute decisions. You can't go back and tinker with them here and there. It either doesn't really make any difference or it just makes things worse.'

Jules looked at Franklin. The lunatic Franklin was having a rest. This was the wise, the old and the little-bit-tired Franklin. Suddenly Jules had a sense of someone struggling to do something much bigger and much harder than just what seemed obvious. It seemed right that if you could see what was wrong and go and fix it up, you would. It was much harder to leave the past alone. To deal with its consequences in your own life and times instead.

'OK, what's her name?'

'Sarah,' said Jules.

'Sarah,' said Franklin. 'Have you ever been to London?'

Sarah's eyes went wide as she shook her head.

'No?' said Franklin. 'Well, you're about to go there quite quickly. I know it'll be a bit disconcerting for a day or two, but I'm sure you'll find your way about. Better than being turned into charcoal, eh?'

Sarah looked ready to cry and Franklin quickly moved on.

'You'll be all right, Sarah, I promise.'

Franklin tapped at the JumpMan on his arm, looked up at Sarah and she disappeared.

'That's it?' asked Jules. 'You're going to throw her into the middle of a city?'

'Jules, big cities are always full of young girls and boys making their own way in the world. Not everyone gets to be tucked up in bed every night. She'll be fine.'

Jules leant back on the fence. He was feeling angry and frustrated. He was starting to feel tired from the weekend, and exhausted from Jumping to the dinosaurs and to the Witch Burning. Two Jumps they'd done. How many millions would they have to do, before they came across Gen?

'Jules?' Theo was trying to get his attention. 'Next Jump. Let's go.'

Jules dragged himself up.

Theo grabbed him by the arm, pressed the GoButton and they were gone.

ZONE ▶ Basic NanoTechnology for Students
ITEM ▶ 2345454-326-65544/BNt356
DIEW ▶ Elementary Nanobot Exercise #5

This is not a dot. This is a Bot. Quite a large Nanobot. Unfortunately this Nanobot is turned off, otherwise you could use it to move atoms around. Well, not atoms – a Nanobot this large (several millions of atoms across) would be too clumsy to handle a single atom. For that you need a Bot about as big as this,

But it's a bit hard to see that Bot. Ask the Walls to make a Scanning Electron Microscope and then you can see it. Write down what it's doing.

Basic NanoTechnology

FOR STUDENTS

chapter seven
Time Limit

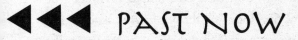 **PAST NOW**

TUESDAY AFTERNOON ◀ EARLY MIL 1

The tremors had ceased and the sky had cleared a little. The birds who'd hid their heads under their wings returned to pecking for worms.

Lavinia's mother had found Gen and Lavinia outside by the wall. She'd grabbed Lavinia by the arm and dragged her back inside. Gen she'd slapped across the head and pointed back towards the kitchen.

Gen had hurried away to avoid further blows, but halfway back across the courtyard she noticed something on her arm. It was a small fleck of grey ash.

She looked at it, and as she did it was joined by another.

Gen stopped. She had to get out of here. Out of this house and out of this town. This was Pompeii, and it was about to be buried.

But what about the family? Everyone at the party? She wanted to warn them, but she couldn't even speak the language. And as if they'd listen to a slave girl!

Gen looked down at her tunic and flimsy sandals. She had an idea. They may not listen to a slave girl, but they might listen to a girl from the future.

She headed back down the corridor to Lavinia's little sleeping room. She took off the tunic and sandals and changed into her own clothes and shoes. Immediately she felt better.

When Gen strode in the guests were all talking excitedly about the earthquake, pointing at the cracks in the walls and speculating on what kind of an omen this would be for the marriage. But they gradually fell silent as they caught sight of the strangely dressed girl.

Gen walked purposefully towards Lavinia, who was standing with her mother.

'Lavinia,' said Gen loudly.

Lavinia turned and her mother gazed at Gen with mixed astonishment and loathing. What was this thing who dared to appear in this outlandish costume to further ruin the day?

'You must go!' Gen declared loudly. 'The volcano is about to blow. You're all going to be killed. We've got to get out of here.'

The guests fell back, pulling away from Lavinia, her mother and Gen. They couldn't understand what she was saying, but some were starting to feel that the omens were very bad indeed. First an earthquake and then an oddly dressed creature speaking in a strange tongue. Time to go perhaps.

'You must understand. I know what's going to happen. It's time to run away!' Gen said loudly.

One or two people discretely ducked out the front door, but most stayed where they were. Perhaps this was some new style of entertainment dreamt up by the family for the wedding.

'You must run,' Gen tried again. 'You will all be covered in lava and mud and dirt and stuff. And then in two thousand years we dig you up and find you. You've got to flee.'

Lavinia's father came over to Gen. He stared at her. And then he barked some orders over her shoulder.

Two burly slaves came and grabbed Gen's arms.

The father stared at her some more and then slapped her full in the face.

'No,' said, Gen starting to sob. 'You must listen to me.'

Lavinia's father raised his hand again. Gen cowered, waiting for the blow.

It didn't come. She looked up. Lavinia had grabbed her father's arm. And now, standing with Lavinia's father was an older man, a servant, perhaps, judging by his clothes, but someone with some kind of authority.

The father looked furious, but he didn't seem as though he was about to hit Gen again immediately.

The older man stepped forward and started talking to Gen. He seemed to be saying things in different languages, but all Gen could do was shake her head. She didn't understand any of it.

The old man stopped and looked around at Lavinia's father. He seemed to be waiting for orders to continue.

'Gen!' Lavinia yelled out.

'Yes!' said Gen. 'I'm Gen. Gen. Gen.'

The older man turned back to her. 'Gen,' he said, pointing at her.

Patting himself on the chest, he said slowly, 'Claudius.'

Gen nodded and repeated again quickly, 'Gen. Yes. Gen. You Claudius. Hello, bonjour, 'ow ya doin', wassup?'

Claudius pointed at her and then waved a hand around. He said something that sounded like one word with a question. Was he asking where, where from?

Gen shook her head. 'No,' she said.

'Non!' said Claudius quickly.

'No!' said Gen, smiling a little.

'Non,' said Claudius, also smiling and nodding his head.

'Non!' Gen said again, nodding as well.

Somehow they had a word in common. Across worlds, cultures and centuries, they'd found a word they shared. They both stared at one another for a moment.

It made no sense to Claudius. The Gauls didn't sound like that, no one from Carthage or Alexandria sounded like that. No one in the Roman world sounded anything like it, but there was this word that was virtually the same.

Gen wondered if there might be others.

The guests also looked amazed. Some clapped. This was a marvellous show. So realistic. So clever of Lavinia's parents to devise such a thing. Highly original to ask an actor to play a slave. Or was this a particularly clever slave? That old teacher was very funny in the part as well. And look at the clothes on the young girl. Marvellous!

Gen looked around hopelessly. Some more ash drifted onto her arm. She flicked it off onto the floor, where she noticed that more had already settled.

She looked up through the open roof at the sky. Pieces of ash were starting to swirl in the air.

The guards had loosened their grip a little and she wriggled free.

This time she just addressed Claudius. 'The mountain! The volcano! It's going to go.' The name of the volcano suddenly came to her. 'Vesuvius. Vesuvius. Vesuvius!'

That got everyone's attention.

'Vesuvius?' Claudius asked.

She nodded and then made an exploding noise and flung her arms up in the air. 'Vesuvius,' she said again.

That was enough. Panic gripped the room. This was no show. This was a prophet, an oracle, a messenger from the gods. Time to go. Someone screamed and everyone ran for the door.

Claudius' eyes had opened wide and he stared at her. Lavinia's father looked around hopelessly as the guests started pushing their way out. Her mother glared at Gen with deep hatred for ruining the wedding.

Gen grabbed Lavinia by the wrist and they ran back into the house, across the courtyard, past the kitchen, through a gate and out into the street.

Lavinia stopped still, and turned towards the house. 'My mother! My family,' she cried.

It was Gen's turn to comprehend without understanding the words. 'We've got to get away from here!' she shouted, grabbing Lavinia, and together they ran into the main street and headed downhill. Gen had no real idea where to go, but downhill at least was easier and it was away from the mountain.

It only took a few minutes to reach the bay. As they ran onto the beach, there was an ear-splitting noise.

They turned and looked back at Vesuvius. Great sheets of flame were leaping from the top of the mountain, up into the thick clouds that were gathered around its top. Smoke and ash filled the sky like ink, blotting out the sun. The day went suddenly dark.

Gen and Lavinia fell onto the sand, not sure where to run next. Gen felt the air thicken with heat. If she breathed through her nose she was sickened by the foul stench in the air; if she breathed through her mouth it burnt the back of her throat. She started to cough.

Lavinia's eyes were streaming with tears and with the sting of hot dust and ash.

Gen stood and hauled her up. 'We've got to keep going,' she yelled. 'We'll die here!'

Ash was starting to fall like heavy snow. Gen brushed it off and began to run along the beach with Lavinia. She only got a few metres before another tremor shook the earth. Falling to the ground she closed her eyes in terror, waiting for the tremors to pass. When she opened them she saw the sea had been sucked away from the shore, leaving the sea floor exposed. Damp weeds and plants were shrivelling quickly in the heated air. Fish flopped once or twice before lying still.

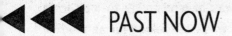

LATE AFTERNOON WEDNESDAY ◄ LATE MINUS
MIL 1 (184 BC, OLD TIME)

Jules opened his eyes and had to shut them again. He was standing in brilliant sunshine and it was unbearably bright. He and Theo squinted and blinked for a full minute until their eyes adjusted and they could look about them. It was warm, and the air was full of the scent of lavender and jasmine. There was a salty tang as well. They must be somewhere near the ocean. They were on a cobbled road that ran up towards the top of a hill. Here and there stood some squat stone buildings. Some looked like houses; some like shops.

This was a lot nicer than some squalid mediaeval village. But so what? thought Jules. He couldn't help feeling an overwhelming sense of frustration. This can't be enough. He and Theo and the girls Jumping off to a few different sites, hoping they might run into Genevieve walking up the track towards them. Sometimes he went to school and didn't run into her all day. What were the chances they'd Jump to somewhere and there'd she'd be? How many places could they get to? Would they just go on looking for ever?

It was hopeless. It was beyond trying to look for a needle in a haystack. It was like looking for an atom of a needle on a planet of haystacks. And he was the only one worried about it. Theo and Franklin were acting like this was really going to work.

At that moment, instead of slumping down on a marble kerb in despair, Theo, as usual, was mainly concerned with his costume. The Coat was alternating between a long flowing white robe and a shortish cream tunic.

'What do you think, Jules?' Theo asked, oblivious to Jules' anguished look. 'The robe or this top here? The long robe might get a bit warm, I think.' Jules looked up at him, disbelieving. Theo's hair was turning white.

'Do you even care?' Jules asked.

'Care? Of course I care. We must get our appearance right.'

'I don't mean about that! I mean about Gen? Do you actually care about trying to find Gen?'

'Yip! Surely do. What's got into you?'

Jules shoulders slumped and gestured around. 'This. Us. Everything. What's the use? We're never going to find her.'

'Well, Jules, we'll never find her with that attitude, that's for sure.'

'You're as bad as my brain. Where are we, anyway?'

'Crete, the Labyrinth JumpSite,' said Theo. 'I've been here before.' Theo looked at him. 'We have to keep looking, Jules.'

Jules shook his head.

'C'mon, let's be quick. Let's find the Labyrinth and get going.'

They turned and started walking up through the town. It really was a beautiful day, and it was hard not to feel better with this warm gentle sun on your face. People smiled at them as they went by. Jules felt a little conspicious in his modern clothes, but Theo's Coat had now fully adjusted itself to local conditions. He'd decided on the tunic, his purple shoes were sandals, and his hair, although it was a rather startling white, was at least white all over with nothing flashing or zapping about.

They reached a row of shops and Theo stopped in front of the first. It sold pots and pans and kitchenware. 'Good morrow, good fellow. Good tidings this day?' Theo tried a bit more of his old-fashioned language.

The good fellow looked up, startled, and said, 'Hocleun Phillgoel, ig noig?' Or something that sounded like that.

Theo kept on smiling and muttered to his Coat, 'Translation?'

The collar of the Coat discretely rose to Theo's ear and in a low tone, which Jules could just catch, said,

'He appears to be speaking ancient Cretan. He said, "Who the hell are you?" You should reply,' and the Coat told Theo how to say Good morning, I'm sorry to interrupt you, but could you direct me to the Labyrinth? in ancient Cretan.

The man's face went pale. He pointed in the direction of the white stone temple at the top of the hill and then scurried back inside his shop, suddenly very interested in polishing the bottom of a large bronze jug.

Theo shrugged and they continued up the hill towards the temple.

It seemed deserted when they got there.

Jules called out a tentative 'Hello?'

There was no response.

They walked over to a statue of a woman riding a bull. Theo grabbed a flaming torch off one wall and held it up. They could now see the entrance to a cave.

'The Labyrinth?' said Theo.

'I suppose so,' said Jules.

~ *You're going in?* inquired his brain.

~ *Yes.*

~ *You know what Labyrinth means, don't you?*

~ *It's like a maze.*

~ *No. Maze suggests summer afternoons and cucumber sandwiches and after half an hour of amusing fun you come out again and perhaps play croquet on the lawn.*

Labyrinth suggests dark tunnels underground designed to lose you forever, until the next unfortunate stumbles in and finds your bones. I was very quiet with the dinosaurs and you hardly heard me at all with those weird men with hot pokers and you know how I feel about pain. But can we skip this?

~ And just leave Gen in here?

~ *Well, that's my point,* said his brain. *I don't know why you think she's going to be somewhere like this. Quincy is a criminal mastermind. He'd send her to the last place any of you would ever look. These are the first places you're going to look. Why not go straight to the last place?*

This made a lot of sense to Jules, but as soon as he tried to explain it, it didn't. 'Theo! Let's not worry about the Labyrinth. Let's go to the last place we think Gen will be!'

'The last place? What do you mean?'

'Well, isn't that exactly where she's going to be? "The last place we'll ever think of." That's where we need to go, and we need to go there now!'

'Doesn't make sense. You can't think of the last thing first. You have to think of the first things first, and then you'll think of the last thing.'

'Why?'

'Well, if you think of it next, then it's not going to be the last place you can think of, is it? It's going to be the next place you can think of.'

'But you see what I mean, don't you? If we could think right now of the last place we can think of, think of all the places we wouldn't have to think of.'

Theo turned to look at Jules. 'You know, it's funny, Dodoboy, but I don't usually have trouble understanding what you're talking about. That's usually your problem with me.'

'But you know what's going to happen. We'll find her, and we'll say, "Oh my God, I can't believe she's there! That's the last place I would have thought of." Can't we at least try to think of it first?'

Theo shrugged and they stopped for a moment. 'Thought of anything yet?' Theo asked after a minute or two.

Jules shook his head and they turned and walked into the cave.

Theo held up the torch. The cave quickly turned into a passage with a smooth floor and walls that ran steeply down. They set off down the passageway and soon they couldn't see the entrance at all.

A few steps further and they came to an intersection. 'Left or right?' asked Jules.

'Wip, that's the whole thing with labyrinths,' observed Theo. 'You can either try to decide which way to go and really think about it, or you can just choose the first way you think of. Either way, you're going to get lost.'

'Get lost?'

'It's what a labyrinth is for. It's to lose people in. That's why we're looking here. Maybe Quincy wanted Gen to get lost here.'

'So for us to find her, we'll have to get lost in the same place as her.'

'Yip, that's about it.'

Jules was getting tired. He'd hardly slept all weekend. He'd completely lost track of the day, which seemed to have way too many hours in it. And Theo was starting to annoy him. He was so chirpy about it all, like they'd just bound around the corner and there she'd be. It was really getting on his nerves.

They turned left and a few steps further on there was another passage. They spent a moment choosing and set off again. Now every few steps there was another tunnel, or fork, or three tunnels splitting off with one going up, one going down and one going straight ahead. They began to choose at random.

They were now well and truly lost. Jules was stricken with an overwhelming desire to turn and run. He wanted to go back outside, to the sun and the wind, where he could take deep breaths and smell the jasmine in the air. 'What is that smell, Theo?'

'Which smell? Do you mean the grainy one, or the cold-air one, or the rank, stale, meaty one that hits you in the back of the throat?'

That last one was bad.

'What is this place?' asked Jules. 'Why is it here?'

'To scare young TimeJumpers!' said Theo. 'Nip, it's where the Minotaur lives.'

'The what?'

'The Minotaur. Big scary thing with the body of a man and the head of a bull. Lives in here and gobbles up virgins, whenever they're sacrificed to him.'

Jules stopped. 'Are you serious? We are just walking blindly through all these tunnels, and around the corner we might run into that?'

'Oh come on Jules, zif. Body of a man and the head of a bull. What do you think it lives down here with? A unicorn?'

Jules exploded. 'What is it with you? You just keep joking around. I don't care if there's a Minotaur down here or Winnie the Pooh. I want to find Gen. If she's here, she's in danger. She'll be lost. She'll be stuck here. She doesn't have a JumpMan, remember?'

Theo kicked his sandals a little in the dust. 'Hip, Jules. I'm worried too. But you're too uptight. How do you think like that?'

Jules lashed out and punched Theo in the face.

Theo stood there, horrified, a little drop of blood oozing from a cut on his lip. 'You hit me?' he said.

'Yeah, I hit you,' yelled Jules. 'What, don't they hit in

your Now? Is that another thing that's really dumb about Mil 3?' And Jules gave Theo a shove.

~ *This anger thing. I can' t really help you with it,* said Jules' brain.

~ *Shut up!*

'Nip, we know about punching,' said Theo quietly, and he stepped forward and landed a quick one on Jules' cheek.

The boys leapt at one another, and Theo dropped the torch on the ground. They wrestled furiously in the darkness, punching and grabbing.

Then they pulled apart, and Theo picked up the torch, which had nearly gone out. It flared up again. They stood breathing heavily, glaring at each other.

'Jules,' said Theo. 'I think you'd better calm down. This isn't helping us find Gen.'

Jules was still too fired up. 'Yeah, right. You're just too gutless. Pooncey little future kid. Can't take it.'

'No, that's not it . . .' said Theo, quickly looking over Jules' shoulder.

'Oh yeah? Well, come on then. You want to go again? Think you can take me?'

'Ahh, Jules.' Theo was pointing over Jules' shoulder.

'Are you serious? You want me to turn around? So you can jump on me, when I'm not looking? You think I'm that stupid?'

'Jules, seriously, behind you . . .' Theo backed away a little.

'Oh, what is it?' said Jules in a teasing voice. 'A big scary Minotaur?' and he took a quick glance over his shoulder.

Filling up the whole passage was a massive pair of horns. The horns were sprouting from the head of a bull. Its eyes were flaring red, and smoke was pouring from its nostrils. As Jules met the gaze of the bull, it snorted and lowered its horns ominously. Jules couldn't speak.

The thing came slowly towards him. Jules took a few steps backwards towards Theo.

'Jules get behind me!' Theo yelled.

Theo leapt forward and thrust the torch right into the monster's face.

It stumbled backwards, cracking its head on the Labyrinth wall. Jules heard a very human-sounding 'Ouch!'

Theo grinned and thrust the torch forward once more.

The bull stumbled again and fell over completely. Its head rolled off and down the passage a metre or two.

'Who dares to wake the Minotaur?' came a squeaky voice from the floor of the passage. 'Begone, or my curse will be on you.' Theo's Coat did some quick translating.

'Seen a girl anywhere around here?' asked Theo, holding up the torch as he walked towards the voice.

Jules followed Theo, and he could now see that the

bull's head was a cleverly made mask. The eyes were just polished stones reflecting the light of the torch, and a little pot of coals was making all the smoke.

'A girl? No,' said the man. 'Why aren't you running for your lives? Who are you?'

'Wip, it's pretty obvious why we're not running, wouldn't you say?' said Theo. 'I might run from the Minotaur, but I'm not that scared of a guy in a Minotaur mask.'

'How did you know?'

'Lucky guess,' said Theo, helping the man up and dusting him down.

'You won't tell anyone?' he said. 'It's a good job. I can work my own hours. And my brother-in-law does nights, so I don't want to wreck it.'

'Nip, relax. We're not going to tell anyone. We're just looking for someone. Girl about our age? Straight hair, possibly wearing quite strange clothes?'

The man shook his head.

'Could she be wandering around out there in the Labyrinth somewhere?' asked Jules.

Again the man shook his head. 'No. Doesn't really matter which tunnel you choose, they all end up in the same place. It just seems really confusing because it's dark.'

Jules started to feel hopeless again. 'What are we doing here?' he said to Theo. 'This is just a joke. We're wasting time.'

Theo sighed, nodded and checked the JumpMan.

'You won't tell anyone? You promise?' the man asked again.

'Your secret is safe for all time,' replied Theo and he pressed the GoButton on his JumpMan.

They were back at school. Jules cast an angry look at Theo then stomped off. He needed a moment to calm down and think. This was hopeless. Where would they go next? Coney Island? Perhaps she's trapped in the ghost train.

School was over and the students were going home. At the bus stop out the front they jostled and yelled as they threw their bags into cars or climbed onto buses. They checked messages on their phones and promised to call one another in half an hour.

Jules leant against the gate and rubbed his face with his hands. What was going to happen now?

What would happen when Gen didn't come home from school?

What was he going to tell her parents?

'Jules?' said a voice. It sounded far away. He took his hands away from his face and in front of him, standing behind an open car door, was his mother.

'Jules, is that you?'

Jules didn't react. He'd forgotten about his mother. He'd forgotten that his dad had said she was going to pick him up. His mother. He hadn't seen her for three months and had had no time today to think about the fact that she was coming back.

Coming back here to live. Coming back here with . . . with – well, he didn't really want to think about that aspect of the whole thing right now.

He recovered and waved slightly, trying to summon up a smile from somewhere.

She closed the car door and started towards him.

Jules felt someone grab his elbow.

'There you are,' snapped Franklin. 'Theo tells me you're losing heart. Why?'

Jules looked over at his mother, who'd stopped, a little puzzled by the sudden appearance beside her son of a dirty, skinny old man.

And then, right in front him, Bonnie reappeared. 'God, those druids are nasty!' she exclaimed. 'You do not want to stand between them and a lunar eclipse! Hi Jules.' Bonnie had never been so friendly. 'Where next?'

'I've never known why but everyone always wants to go to Timbuktu,' said Franklin. 'Quincy was no exception. Loved the place. Go!'

Bonnie disappeared.

'So what's up with you?' Franklin turned his attention back to Jules.

Jules could see his mother still looking at them both, but this time she had her hand over her mouth and had gone quite pale.

Jules squirmed a little under Franklin's gaze, but then spoke up. 'What chance have we got, Franklin? She could be anywhere, and we're dropping in on one little place at a time. We've only made it to about three places today!'

Kyeela reappeared at Franklin's elbow.

'Oh do not send me to any more sailing ships!' she whined. 'Those sailors are horrible! They're all mad, their breath is putrid, half of them wanted to throw me overboard, half of them wanted to eat me!' She shuddered at the memory. 'Could I go to a city next?'

'Sure,' said Franklin. 'Shanghai, 1852. Terrific city! Bye!'

'Great!' she said and pressed the button on her JumpMan and disappeared.

'No one else is complaining!' said Franklin as Sonja popped up.

'Man, those Neanderthals hate us Homo Sapiens. Really, really hate us. Can I go somewhere a little less hostile, please?' She grinned at Jules. 'Love this TimeJumping!'

'Bye!' yelled Franklin, and off she went as well.

Jules' mother was leaning back on her car, massaging her temples. She was trying to get up to come over but her legs wouldn't carry her.

Jules stared down at the ground.

'Look at those girls,' said Franklin. 'This morning they could barely tell the time. Now they've been to fifteen Sites each! Maybe I should split you and Theo up. Cover more ground.'

'It's hopeless, Franklin!' yelled Jules. 'Why do you keep pretending? You, you of all people should know. You were at a JumpSite that everyone went to every day and no one found you for years. You know how many Sites there are now? And we're just guessing that Quincy has sent her somewhere dramatic. He might have sent her to the middle of an Idaho potato field the day before yesterday. She doesn't have to be in an earthquake or underneath a tsunami or standing in the middle of a lava flow while the volcano explodes . . .'

~ *I've got it!* said his brain.

~ *What? What have you got? Tell me what you've got?*

~ *Don't squeeze it! It's there.*

Jules had gone silent. He stared at his mother as she crawled back into her car and slumped behind the wheel.

'Jules?' said Franklin.

Jules held up a hand.

~ *Tsunami?* he asked his brain.

~ *No! Just let me find it. You said lava flow.*

'Hip, Franklin. I'm just wondering if maybe Jules and I should split up.' Theo had found them.

Franklin waved at him to be quiet.

Jules stared straight ahead, watching his mother in the front seat of her car scrabbling around for her bag.

~ *Volcano?*

~ *Volcano,* agreed his brain.

~ *I've got it!*

'I've got it,' said Jules quietly. 'I know the place. I know where she is. I just don't know the date. How can I find out the date?'

'Ask the Coat!' yelled Theo, leaping over to Jules and grabbing him by the arm.

Two seconds later, Theo pressed the GoButton and the boys disappeared.

In the front seat of her car, Angela Santorini sat frozen, her mobile phone halfway to her ear.

ZONE ► MetroOne BulSheet
ITEM ► 56187BR-RRR-312654410/BUL915
VIEW ► THEODORE PINE FOUR STORY #568

MetroOne

2.15 pm, 7 July

Fifteen Billion and Seventy-three

Four and half minutes ago, Theodore Pine Four, TimeJumper Numero Uno, Starlicker and student, revealed his latest hairstyle. In a stunning departure from his usual brightly coloured and vigorous designs, Theodore Pine's hair was a dullish dark brown. As he walked from the Academy to a StretchPod, Theodore informed BulSheet's awaiting Theo correspondent: 'This is my natural colour. I'd been using Molecule Follicle Gel for so long, I'd forgotten what I actually looked like. It's weird – even though it's me, I don't think it's very me.'

Theo moved off, accompanied by personal assistant Honeydew Meloni, who was anxiously apologising for not having a jar of Gel handy. It is expected that by 2.30 pm, Eastern Metro Time, Theo will reveal a new style focusing on issues and relevant to today's young TimeJumpers.

chapter eight
The Test of Time

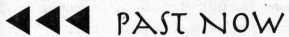 PAST NOW

LATE AFTERNOON, TUESDAY ◄ EARLY MIL 1

Gen hunched over. If she made herself into a ball she could breathe a little more easily. The air now smelt putrid, and all around her ash was falling. It floated, soft, fatal down. She was surprised how heavy it became once a layer or two of it built up on her shoulders or legs. The air burnt her throat as she breathed it in. She tried to create a mask with her shirt but it didn't seem to make much difference.

The mountain was continually exploding but at least here they felt safe from falling buildings. Gen had hoped they might be able to get on a boat and sail away from all this destruction, but the sea was boiling away about two or three hundred metres out from where it should have been. The strange sea, the clouds that billowed and rolled above them, the stench, the dying fish – everything made it seem like this was the end of the world.

Lavinia was crying for her family. Gen's eyes were streaming as well. She was almost paralysed with fear; she wanted her own family. This was it, this was where it was going to end. She'd never see them again, she'd never grow up. This was as old as she'd ever be.

Lavinia hugged her fiercely, and they both pressed their faces into the sand. That felt cool, and for a moment they could gulp some air free from the falling ash.

Then it felt like the sky had come down to meet the earth. There was a crackling all around them, a kind of electricity in the air, and forks of lightning snapped out of the dark clouds, cracking open trees and lighting up the crumbling streets. Gen stole a look at Vesuvius. Its side had opened up as if it were made of cheap paper. Red flames leapt forth and hot gold lava bubbled out and began to pour down the mountain. In minutes the first flows began to curl around the outskirts of the town.

Hundreds of years in the future all this would be dug up again. The houses and the people would all be found, preserved just as they are now. A world interrupted and then immediately buried. A town trying to escape, a town full of people caught before they realised what was happening. Some people didn't get out of their chairs. Some people ran to hug their children and that's how they were found.

It must all happen so quickly, thought Gen, that they can't escape, can't let the dogs off their chains, can't do anything much except hold one another and cry like she and Lavinia were doing now.

Would they be found? A poignant tableau, two young girls comforting one another at the end? Best friends or sisters, everyone will think.

Gen shivered at the thought. Why was this happening to her? What had she done? Why hadn't she believed Franklin? It was obvious now that Quincy was trying to kill her. He hadn't sent her to the future. He'd sent her here, to die in history's most famous time capsule, a horrible kind of TimeJumping joke.

Why?

She closed her eyes, feeling not sleepy so much but as though her mind was slipping away from her. As though it was now floating off somewhere all on its own and was turning around to look at her. Is this death, she wondered, and her mind answered, not yet. Don't let me die here, she said to her mind. I want to see my mother, my father. I even want to see Cynthia. Where's Theo – why doesn't he care enough to come and find me? What's happened to Jules? Surely he must realise something's wrong ... Thoughts kept tumbling around in her head and soon Gen could no longer really tell if she was asleep or awake, alive or dead.

The JumpSite moved the moment Jules and Theo arrived in Pompeii. The street subsided and buckled as if it was a sloppy water bed. Jules fell over and wasn't sure if he'd be able to stand up again.

Theo was sprawled in the mud. He'd been knocked over by a fleeing goat, which had butted straight into him at full speed as soon as he'd appeared. He picked himself up and immediately started complaining. 'I don't believe this. The Romans were filthy. You know what this brown muck in the street is, don't you? It's shit. Human shit. They just let it pour away down the middle of everything. It's all over me, and I'm sorry, but you really stink, Jules, because you are standing right in the middle of it. And they call this civilisation.'

Theo's Coat leapt into action. 'Suggest immediate

JumpOut, Theo! Seismic readings indicate volcanic activity. Atmospheric readings indicate sulphur, carbon monoxide and a range of other gases not intended for breathing. Activating NanoClean immediately. In fact, all resources are being deployed to clean Coat because whatever it is you landed in is really disgusting. Just running routine TimeChecks now.'

The Coat then sounded an ear-splitting alarm. 'WARNING WARNING. YOU ARE NOW IN PROHIBITED JUMPSITE. YOU HAVE STAYED TOO LONG! AUG 24, AD 79 IN OLD TIME, IS THE DESTRUCTION OF POMPEII. IN TWO HOURS' TIME, POMPEII WILL GO UNDER. UNLESS YOU WOULD LIKE TO STAY HERE UNTIL 1768 OLD TIME, WHEN EXCAVATIONS BEGIN, SUGGEST IMMEDIATE JUMPOUT.'

'What do you think, Jules, should we go?'

Jules looked up at Theo in astonishment. 'She's here! I'm sure she's here.'

'Sure, but where?'

Jules looked at the scene around them and saw what Theo meant. People were fleeing, trying to get back home. Children were crying, animals bleating and stampeding – it was pandemonium. It was dark, it stank, and they both started to cough from breathing in the ash-laden air. If Gen was here she was going to be hard to find.

'We're still not sure she's even visible.'

Jules grabbed Theo. 'Shut up!' he screamed. 'She's here. Let's start looking!'

They began to push through the crowd.

Some people were going back into their houses.

Jules wanted to shout at them to keep moving, to get away. He did, but it just sounded like more panicked screaming. Theo got the Coat to translate 'Let us through, please,' and 'Excuse me' into Latin, but that didn't make much difference.

Jules tried to look at everyone they passed. Is that her? Is that her? He attempted to keep fear at bay. What if she's just inside that house there? What if she's just in the next street? How are they ever going to look everywhere? What if she's not even visible?

The crowd thinned out a little as people turned to take the road out of town and others continued down towards the bay. Jules and Theo followed them.

They started yelling out her name. 'GENNNNN! GEEEEENNNNNNNN!'

No one answered. No one offered to help. No one could do anything except look after themselves. Everyone's world was collapsing around their ears. Everyone needed help.

The boys ran on, darting up alleys and sometimes running into homes. They came to the end of the street, where it widened out to meet the shore.

Something didn't look quite right. The sea didn't seem to be where it should be and there were dead fish lying around. The beach was full of people. Some that could still move were trying to get the attention of boats out on the water. But most were just sitting exhausted, in shock or unable to function in the poisonous air.

Jules and Theo ran down, slower now as they, too, started to succumb to the gases that were pouring out of the mountain. Theo doubled over quickly, unable to breath. Jules supported him and they walked out onto the beach to look for Gen.

Gen felt her mind getting further and further off. It was saying, don't worry, don't worry, but it sounded like it was a long way away. It was reassuring her. If this is the end, it's not too bad, is it? There's no pain and in a minute or two you'll slip under and that will be that. Think of all the things you'll never have to worry about now. School. Your mother. Getting away from Cynthia. Deciding what to do about Jules or Theo. As Gen had that thought, she had the strangest sensation. She felt as though she could hear someone calling her name. Like the messages from her mind, it sounded very far off. Who could be calling her name here? Who in the final hours of Pompeii knew her?

Who from anywhere else in the vast reaches of Time knew she was here?

No one.

So more dreams. And it must be part of the dream, she thought, that it sounds like Jules and Theo that are calling her name. Funny how your mind works. Still, at least this was a nice dream. It would be nice to think that the boys had come to look for her. She snuggled a little further into the sand and then a tiny prompt came from her mind as it was about to wander off for ever.

It could be the boys, you know. Maybe, they're here. Just take a look.

Jules ran up and down the beach. Theo walked slowly, but his hair was now blinking bright red like an emergency beacon and his Coat was broadcasting at full volume. 'GEN!' it repeated. 'COME TOWARD US. IT'S US, THEO AND JULES. GEN, GEN, GEENNNNNNN!'

Jules was working hard to stop a desperate panicking feeling from taking over. He was working so hard at it he nearly missed what his brain was trying to tell him.

~ *Let me through, I've got something. It's coming in from Peripheral.*

~ *What? WHAT?*

~ *Stop yelling for a moment, will you? You know how sometimes you see things, and then it takes you a moment to realise you've seen it and sometimes you weren't even really looking at it and sometimes you have to take a moment to figure out what it was you saw?*

~ *Yeah?*

~ *It's one of those.*

Jules brain paused for what seemed like forever.

~ *Thirty degrees right! Those two girls! One of them is just putting her head back in the sand. She was looking straight at you. I'm getting a match now. Hold on . . .*

Gen raised her head just a little. She could see a young boy in jeans and T-shirt. A little way beyond him she saw another young boy with hair that was flashing red on and off. He also had a Coat and her name was lit up all over it. Someone was calling out to her, over and over again.

This is so good, she thought. Not only am I imagining I'm hearing things, but I'm seeing things as well. That's so nice. At least my last thoughts will be happy. Smiling, she lay her head back down in the sand.

A few seconds later she felt someone thud down beside her, and gently turn her over. Gen squinted as some ash fell onto her face, and coughed as she breathed in the burning air once more.

Whoever it was yelled something out. 'Theo!' it sounded like. 'She's here!'

Suddenly there were two faces looking down at her. 'Gen?' they both asked. 'Are you all right?'

She smiled dreamily at them. This is great, she thought. Really, this is great. In fact this is so great, I'm going to pretend it's real and I'm going to talk to them.

Jules and Theo leaned in closer as Gen began to whisper. 'You're both here,' she said. 'That's great. I love you, Theo. I love you, Jules. You're the best friends a girl could have, even if you are a complete wanker, Theo, and even if you haven't the faintest idea what to do, Jules. You're both great.' And she smiled some more at them and closed her eyes.

Jules and Theo looked at her with deep concern. 'She's obviously sick,' said Theo.

'Badly,' agreed Jules. 'She doesn't know what she's saying.'

'Time to go,' said Theo, and he rolled up his sleeve to get to his JumpMan.

As he did so, Jules felt someone tugging on his shirt. It was the girl who'd been hugging Gen when they arrived. She spoke, but Jules couldn't understand what she was saying.

'Theo,' he said. 'Can you translate?'

While Theo was getting the Coat to translate, Jules was trying to get Gen to sit up. She seemed almost unconscious.

'She's saying, I want to get back to my family,' translated the Coat.

'What do we do?' asked Jules. 'Are we going to Jump her?'

'Where?' asked Theo. 'To Mil 3? We just tried that with the witch. What'll Franklin say?'

But Jules wasn't listening. He was staring down at Gen's feet.

Her shoes.

She was wearing her shoes.

She can't be wearing her shoes. Her shoes have to be under the bed.

He'd only thought 'Pompeii!' because of the shoes.

Because of the story he'd read about a pair of modern shoes that were found under a bed in a villa in Pompeii that had been buried under ash and mud for two thousand years. He'd talked about it with Gen the night they went to the movies.

How did the shoes get there? Everyone had wanted to know. He and Gen had laughed about it at the time.

But now Jules was about to provide the answer.

He was going to have to put them there.

'The shoes,' he yelled. 'She's still wearing her shoes!'

Theo looked up, a little annoyed. 'Do you mind? I'm trying to translate and help this girl. Lavinia, I think she said her name was.'

'No!' yelled Jules. 'We can't take the shoes with us. The shoes have to stay here in Pompeii and be buried here.

They have to be found under a bed in my time, and then be in the newspaper so I can read about them, and then ten minutes ago remember them and make the connection with Gen! If they're not there . . .'

Theo understood.

'But where, Jules?' he asked quietly. 'Back in there?'

Theo pointed back at the town. Some streets were now blocked with mud and molten lava. The sky was black with smoke, fire was everywhere, and Vesuvius continued to roar.

'You Jump Gen,' said Jules. 'Then come straight back. We'll take this girl and find her house, put the shoes back and then we'll Jump out of here.'

Theo nodded. He took off his Coat. 'Take it,' he said. 'It's got an air purifying system. It'll help you both. I'll be back in one minute.'

Jules slipped on the Coat and Theo knelt down next to Gen and helped her take off her shoes. He checked the codes on his JumpMan, gave Jules a strange kind of V sign, and then he and Gen disappeared.

Lavinia stared at the spot where Gen had been.

Jules grabbed her by the shoulders and put his face up close to hers. 'Don't worry about that,' he said, and the Coat translated it into Latin.

Lavinia just stared stiffly back at Jules. She was in deep shock now. Barely an hour ago, she'd been reluctantly preparing for a wedding. Now she was kneeling on damp sand, strange boys were yelling at her, her town was being consumed by smoke and flame, and people had started disappearing. It was a bit much.

'Coat!' ordered Jules. 'Air system! We need some clean air here!'

'Right sleeve!' responded the Coat. 'Pull your hand back out and place sleeve over mouth. You should be getting strong blasts of cool filtered air!'

Jules did as he was told then sucked in deeply and gratefully. He felt clearer and stronger.

He helped Lavinia do the same. She sat there, mute, then blinked her eyes rapidly as the cool air took effect.

'Where's your family?' Jules asked. 'Where's your home? Your mother, your father?' The Coat repeated him in Latin.

Lavinia pointed back at the town.

Some large stones thudded onto the beach right by them. Theo suddenly appeared as well.

'She OK?' yelled Jules.

Theo nodded.

'Come on then. We've got to go back to town!'

Jules grabbed Gen's shoes and helped Lavinia up. They all took a deep breath of the filtered air, and then with Theo on the other side, they went as quickly as they could back up the beach to the town.

There were few people about. Either everyone had gone, or perhaps now everyone was trapped. Some places were still standing, but quite a few buildings had collapsed following the earthquakes. Others were on fire. At the first intersection Jules glanced left and saw a bright orange flow of lava coming slowly towards them. It looked quite beautiful, pouring like molten chocolate down some stairs and around a house.

Then a large rock crashed into a wall just near them. They all leapt sideways and Lavinia fell to the ground.

Jules helped her up, and then asked her quietly. 'Where's your home from here? Can you take us?'

The Coat translated. Lavinia nodded. She seemed keen to help. She wanted to find her family, and in her shock it appeared she was no longer noticing the destruction around her.

They followed her up the street that she and Gen had run down earlier.

I could duck in and put the damn shoes under any bed, Jules thought. There was a house right there. Do it now, Jump, it's all over.

But Jules felt sure it had to be the right bed. What if the shoes were discovered before Mil 3? Some old doddery explorer pulls them up, and they never get noticed. Or worse, they are never dug up at all. He could still get it wrong, but he had to try. What else could he do?

Now Jules could see Vesuvius' red and angry peak. Lava was pouring out of fissures and cracks everywhere and smoke billowed out the top. Jules had used the word 'awesome' quite often in his life, but this was perhaps the only moment he'd felt genuine and deep awe. Volcanoes in the movies never looked like this. You didn't get the same sense of unlimited power and destructive energy. You didn't feel the searing heat, smell the sulphurous gases, and see a sky full of thick black smoke, steam and fire all at once.

Definitely awesome.

They turned a corner and Lavinia pointed. 'Here,' the Coat translated, and Jules and Theo followed Lavinia into her house.

It was still standing. Lavinia shouted out.

'Mother! Father!' the Coat translated for Jules.

'Was there a room somewhere, a room that you and Gen were in?' asked Jules. 'A bedroom, maybe?'

Lavinia pointed to an alcove off the courtyard. Jules ran over and shoved the shoes under the low, tiny bed. He turned around but Lavinia had gone.

'Theo!' yelled Jules. 'Where did she go?'

'She ran down there,' said Theo, pointing to some steps that led to a basement, 'and then she came back up, ran past me and out into the street.'

Jules and Theo ran across the courtyard and back out the door.

Lavinia was running quickly down the street.

'Lavinia!' Jules yelled.

She didn't turn around.

'Jules,' said Theo quietly. Jules turned. Everything had gone strangely silent. The mountain still seemed to be roaring, the earth was shaking a little, lumps of molten rock were still crashing about them. But it was as though the air had been sucked out of the street and had taken all the noise with it. Jules saw what Theo was trying to draw his attention to. Rolling in towards them was a giant cloud. It was rolling quite slowly, but it was consuming everything in its path, drawing in all the dust, the ash, the screams and the smoke.

'We've got to go,' said Theo.

Jules could no longer see Lavinia. Why had she run away? He felt Theo grab his arm and then he was gone.

It was amazing how much information about a place you could absorb immediately, Jules thought. From the smells, the sound of cars going by, voices, just from the way the sun felt on his face, Jules knew he was back in Mil 3. The air was fresh and he gulped it down like water.

Sitting on the wall outside the school was Gen. Around her were Sonja, Kyeela and Bonnie. Somehow they looked less monstrous than usual.

Franklin was standing near them, tapping his teeth. He ran over to Jules and Theo as soon as they appeared. He was incredibly excited. 'Yip!' he shouted, jumping into the air. 'You're back. Everyone's back! Rip, you ready? One more thing to do!'

Jules stood up slowly. 'Just hang on a second, Franklin, will you?'

Jules had just noticed that it wasn't only them outside the school. In fact, surrounding them was a ring of about twenty police. As he looked at them, a couple more cars pulled up, sirens wailing. Then a troop of mounted police arrived and stood like cavalry out on the road.

'Yip,' said Franklin. 'I know, you'd like to get your bearings and sort everything out. But no time. And look what your mother's gone and done, Jules. She called the police! There were a couple here to start with and they came over to talk to me, and then, well, everyone started Jumping back in. Every time someone turned up, the police who were here would call more police in. Now look.' Franklin gestured. Police were blocking off the road and moving a crowd away. Helicopters were heading their way as well.

'Jules!'

His mother! Jules looked around and spotted her. She was standing by a police car with a megaphone. Several men in suits were standing behind her, looking nervous.

'Get away from them! Before they make you disappear again! Come over here! You're not going to get into any trouble!'

~ *That always means you are going to get into a lot of trouble. Just not immediately,* said his brain.

Jules' mother's voice had been thin and tearful. He wanted to go. It had been a bit of shock when he'd heard she was coming back, but he missed her and desperately wanted to run over and be hugged by her.

But Franklin stopped him. 'Citizens of the Third Millennium, Old Time!' Franklin's voice suddenly rang out clearly, his Coat assisting. 'Assembled law enforcement officers, Jules' mother, and interested bystanders. I doubt I can explain what has happened here today in any way that could make sense. So I'm not even going to try. Instead, I'm Jumping everyone out of here. A TimeSweep will begin shortly and soon you will have no memory of these events at all. Sorry for the inconvenience. Soneehaha.'

Franklin ducked over and pressed the programming button on the girls' JumpMans.

'Front Entrance, TimeMaster Central. Immediate Present!' he yelled at Theo, who programmed his JumpMan then came and stood next to Jules.

Franklin stood next to Gen.

The police started closing in.

'Now, look here, Mr Franklin,' the most senior one said. 'I'm afraid that if you disappear again, there could be serious consequences.'

'Yip,' said Franklin. 'I hope there will. Let's go!'

They all disappeared.

chapter nine
Time's Up

 FUTURE NOW
THURSDAY AFTERNOON ▶ EARLY FIFTEENTH BILLENNIUM

They landed in a clearing. Through the clearing ran a
Pod rail. On the other side there was a low kind of hill. Just
an ordinary kind of hill, except for the fact that there was a
door in the middle of it. The door was quite ordinary, a plain-
looking, brown kind of door, its plainness underlined by the
brown doormat on the ground in front of it. Printed on the
doormat was the word WELCOME.

They all spoke at once.

'Franklin!' yelled Jules. 'What the hell are you doing?'

'Where are we?' screeched Sonja, Kyeela and Bonnie.

'Oh, no', said Gen. 'No more. Let me go home!'

'Hip!' shouted Franklin. 'Will you stop? We have one more little thing to do and then it's over. We don't do this, we may as well have left Gen to – well, whatever might have happened.'

Gen caught Jules' eye. He smiled at her, and she smiled back.

'Lavinia?' she asked, just mouthing the name.

Jules smile faded and he shook his head.

Gen looked down at the ground.

'Now look', continued Franklin. 'This is the main entrance to TimeMaster Central. Inside is Quincy Carter One. He is the problem and we are the only ones who can fix it. All of us. We need to go in and tell him that we know what he's up to. Oak Eye?'

Sonja looked at the other girls. They didn't seem that impressed.

'Is this the future?' Sonja asked. 'Is this where you're from?'

'Yip', said Franklin. 'Welcome to Fifteen Billion and Seventy-three!'

Sonja raised an eyebrow. 'This? A bit of bush and a door in a hill?'

'Wip, what did you want?'

'I don't know', shrugged Sonja. 'More rockets or something. Big silver towers. This just looks like ... Earth.'

'Well this *is* Earth. You want rockets and things you'll have to go to Mars one day.'

'Mars?' said the girls.

'Later', said Franklin. 'Can we get going?'

'I can't', said Gen, coughing and looking at Frankin with red teary eyes. 'I just want to go home. Now. I've had enough. Really.' Gen bit her lip and Kyeela put an arm around her.

'It was pretty hairy, back there', said Jules. 'Lots of smoke and ash and —' Jules remembered the people in the street and the great cloud that had sucked them all up.

'There was a girl. I think she was Gen's friend. She, umm ...' Again Jules dried up, not really wanting to admit to what may have happened to Lavinia.

Franklin looked around at them, impatient and embarrassed, then clapped his hands. 'Time for everything, people! I know this seems harsh and nasty, but Gen, I need you. We're kind of due right now. We've got to go. Theo, would you mind knocking on the door?'

Theo walked over, stood on the welcome mat and knocked smartly on the door.

A few seconds later the door opened, and they heard a voice call out, 'Yoohoo, Theo's here! And he's not alone!'

'It's no ordinary door', explained Franklin. 'As you knock on it, the door takes samples of your DNA and does retina scans while the doormat weighs you and tiny cameras in the grain of the wood do a body match. By the time you've finished knocking, the door knows who you are and if you're allowed in.'

He marched over and yelled through the open doorway. 'Quincy! You know who it is. And I've got some people with me I think you should meet. Genevieve Corrigan, for example. And Jules. I think you might know them. Couple of their friends.'

The door stayed open.

Franklin jerked his head and they all filed in.

Then everyone forgot they were tired and stressed and exhausted. Because they were standing on an entry platform about the size of a football field. They suddenly felt as if they'd shrunk.

TimeMaster Central, the home of the JumpMan, the JumpMan Pro and all TimeJumping accessories, was an underground space.

A very big space.

Big enough to have a horizon.

Opening out, down and up in a way that made no sense.

~ *I thought we came through a door. But this is just too big. What's holding up the roof?*

Jules understood why his brain was confused. The sheer size of the space seemed impossible. It was like hundreds of cathedrals laid end to end and on top of one another, surrounded by a few dozen football stadiums, all set in the middle of vast open spaces like the Sahara Desert or all of New Mexico.

'Feel like you're in the future now, girls?' asked Franklin.

Sonja just nodded a little, looking around at the smooth metal walls that marched away into the distance on either side.

Gen was staring at some clouds up near what should have been the ceiling, only it was behaving like a sky.

Jules started to see the joke of the ordinary-looking front door. When you can construct something like this, you don't need a big entrance to impress anyone.

'This way,' instructed Franklin, and he walked to the edge of the platform, yelled out 'GoNow!' and stepped off.

He fell, then immediately rose up again. Now he appeared to be floating on something that they couldn't quite see. 'Come on. You'll all need one.'

Jules and the four girls went cautiously over to the edge of the platform and peered over.

It was a very long way down. A very, very long way down. And there was no evidence of what it was a long way down to. It just faded to black.

Franklin was bobbing up and down on nothing. He was standing a bit like a surfer and occasionally he'd whiz around in a tight circle.

'I love these things,' he said.

'Wh-what things?' asked Sonja.

'Ahh, Sonja. Enjoying the future now?' laughed Franklin. 'This is a GoNow. It's just a wing, really. It's made of nothing but Nanobots. It's like you've got billions of tiny jet engines propelling you around. You just steer it with your feet. It's easy!'

'Umm, where are they?'

'Oh, I'm sorry. Mine's invisible. Colour up!' he ordered.

Under his feet appeared a sliver of grey metallic material.

'How do you do that?' asked Jules.

'Bird wings!'

'What?'

'Bird wings. Red bird wings aren't red, they just reflect red, so you see them as red. This is the same, except the Nanos reflect everything, and then they're invisible. Just a gimmick really. Now come on.'

'Come on what?' asked Gen.

'Come on, now. Get on a GoNow and let's go!'

'How do we get on a GoNow?' asked Gen.

'You step off and call "GoNow"! I can't make it any simpler!'

Theo jumped off, yelled 'GoNow!' and then slid into place beside Franklin.

But the Mil 3 kids just couldn't quite bring themselves to take that first step.

Franklin was getting impatient. 'Oh, look, you have to order them up, I can't do it for you. Yell GoNow and step off!'

~ *Ummm. What are you thinking of doing?* asked Jules' brain.

~ *You know what I'm thinking of doing.*

~ *I know I know what you're thinking of doing, I just want to know if you've really thought about it.*

~ *You would know if I'd really thought about it.*

~ *I know I'd know if you'd really thought about it and I know you haven't, so I really want you to.*

~ *Well, if I really think about it, I'm not going to do it, am I?*

~ *That's why I want you to really think about it.*

~ *And then what would we do?*

~ *Well, I don't know, but whatever you did, it wouldn't involve stepping off this platform.*

~ *It worked for Franklin. And Theo.*

~ *How do you know it's going to work for you?*

'GoNow,' Jules said confidently as he stepped off the platform.

There was a moment immediately after stepping off the platform when he felt like he'd just done the last thing he would ever do.

~ *Never have I wanted less than right now to say I told you so.*

And then a moment after that he heard a whooshing sound and something rushed up to meet his feet. It knocked him a little off balance, but then he steadied himself and stood up. Whatever it was raised him gently back until he was level with the platform.

The colour came back to Jules' face.

~ *Can you never ever ever never ever do anything like that again?*

Jules poked around with his foot and found the edges of the platform he was apparently standing on. It was quite large.

He grinned at Gen and the others. 'It works! Colour up!' he said, and a bright orange sliver appeared under his feet.

Eventually they were all out there.

'Rip!' said Franklin. 'Let's go!'

And they shot off at unbelievable speed into the cavernous interior of TimeMaster Central.

~ *Where are we?* asked his brain.

~ *TimeMaster Central,* replied Jules.

~ *Are we inside or outside?*

~ *Inside.*

~ *Are you going to stay around?* Jules inquired.

~ *I don't know,* said his brain. *Blanket over my head on the couch in my office – it's looking pretty good.*

~ *Don't! Don't you dare.*

Jules negotiated with his brain for a while and managed to convince it to hang around unless things got really weird.

Which happened about eight seconds later when they began to pass people who appeared to be floating in mid-air.

They were sitting at desks, holding meetings, talking on communicators, doing work things that seemed similiar to work back in Mil 3. The stark point of difference was that, while the workers were seated, their chairs were invisible. Or they were working at a desk but it wasn't there. Just a computer screen, or a file or a pile of notes, all just sitting on nothing. Their coats hung on hooks that appeared to be attached to nothing. They threw crumpled-up pieces of paper into invisible bins.

'Everyone's going through an invisible phase,' commented Franklin. 'Come back in a week and it'll be fluorescents. Keeps it interesting.'

They whooshed on past meetings, laboratories, sales desks and call centres. People were working above them, below them and all around them. There were no floors or ceilings or hallways or doors. You just took up a spot in the middle of the space and there you were.

These GoNows are great, thought Jules. I really want one. Better than a skateboard, skates, snowboards, any bike, all motorbikes and cars combined.

'If you need to talk, it's Oak Eye,' Jules heard a voice from somewhere. 'I'm fitted with Chat 45.1. I can help you with any problems you might be having in life or work. Please choose from the following options: Affirmations, Empowerment, Self-Realisation, Meditations or Closure.'

'Umm, I'm OK, I guess,' said Jules.

'I'm Oak Eye, you're Oak Eye. That's fine,' continued the GoNow. 'Don't forget we all begin by thinking we're Oak Eye —'

Jules yelled at Theo. 'Can I turn this thing off?'

'Yip. Just say, "Shut up!"'

Jules did, and swooped on in silence. Then he swooped over to swoop along next to Theo.

'Hi.'

'Hi.'

''Sorry about the fight.'

'It's Oh Kay,' said Theo doing a reasonable impression of a Mil 3 accent. 'Primitive people often resort to violence.'

Jules cut him off by bumping his GoNow into Theo's.

'Rip!' said Theo. 'You want to race now?'

Jules crouched lower and the GoNow dropped down and accelerated away.

Theo zipped in behind him.

Franklin yelled at them. 'Down! Down to your right, you zongoids.'

Jules spotted another large platform or terrace, a bit like the one they'd left, and swooped onto it, skidding his GoNow to a perfect stop.

'Beat you!' he yelled at Theo, leaping off and onto the smooth stone floor.

Theo did the same. 'So sad the way you unsophisticated ancient peoples have to compete all the time,' commented Theo as he grabbed Jules and pushed him onto a couch.

'Oh, really?' said Jules, leaping up as the others swooped down to join them.

'Could we save the expressions of friendship via pretend fighting for later?' said Franklin. 'We've got a little job to do now we are here.'

'Where's here?' asked Kyeela.

'Here is Quincy's private apartments. This where he lives. I think he's expecting us. Shall we go through?'

A smoky glass Wall at the back of the terrace slid open. Franklin was right – Quincy *was* expecting them.

They entered a series of rooms, one behind the other. They were crammed with stuff, and not necessarily neatly arranged. One room was packed with musical instruments, another had suits of armour and was laid out like a mediaeval king's banquet hall, with banners, coats of arms, huge horns as goblets and massive knives that looked like you could carve up half a deer with them.

Another room was full of cave paintings, but the paint seemed fresh. A picture of a speared mammoth was brightly coloured.

'You know what's weird about all this?' said Jules. 'It's all new. All this stuff is new.'

'On the spot!' said Franklin. 'Quincy's been happily collecting from the past for years.'

It was strange to see brand new the kind of things you usually saw in a museum or book. The armour sparkled and looked like it had never known a canter around the castle courtyard, let alone a tournament or some war. There was a room of Roman- and Greek-looking statues and they were all in perfect condition. No arms broken off, all noses intact, and some of them brightly painted and highly polished, as if the sculptor had just stood back with his rag to admire his work.

As Jules was pondering this, they walked around a corner and there was Quincy.

'Well, hello,' said Quincy in a warm and welcoming tone. 'Aren't you all looking well. Genevieve, nice to see you again.'

'Don't start getting all smarmy now, Quincy,' said Franklin. 'We're not the board of TimeMaster, we're not your staff, we're not some slobbering audience at the launch of some new fad from you. We are not even UPHIC. We are here to let you know that we know what you're trying to do.'

Quincy smiled and sat down comfortably on a couch shaped like a pair of lips. He motioned for them to sit down too, in some very stylish and comfortable-looking chairs.

'Drinks anyone?' he inquired. 'We have a NanoBar. It'll whip you up anything you like.'

They did all want drinks. It had been thirsty work running around history looking for Gen. And Gen had just realised that somewhere in this endless day she'd missed lunch.

Getting the drinks took some time, as once everyone found they could order absolutely anything, they started to dream up drinks they thought they'd really like.

'Mango Coke, please, but not quite as fizzy as Coke usually is. Perhaps smaller bubbles.'

'I'd like a tea made from herbs but not a really weak kind of tea. Something like an ordinary cup of tea but something that's refreshing like peppermint tea as well.'

'Chocolate milk but with a hint of banana and mint please. Cold but not too cold.'

Drinks finally served, Quincy opened his arms wide in a gesture of friendliness. 'Well, Franklin. What is it? Obviously you've got something to say.'

'You are trying to change history. You are breaking Rule 1. You always wanted to. You always thought we should. And now you are.'

Quincy leaned forward smiling. 'I know. I introduced pizza. Lock me up.'

Franklin looked stern. 'You're doing much more than that. Do you want to explain why you tried to kill this young girl here? Do you want to explain what you're doing in Mil 3? What's your interest in these two?' Franklin pointed towards Jules and Gen. 'What are you really trying to do?'

Quincy sat back and sighed. 'Ahhhh, Franklin. Always so talented and yet so limited. We could have done so much, you and I.' Quincy shrugged. 'What's it matter? I may as well tell you. As you seem to be the only people who care.'

He stood up and addressed them proudly. 'I'm going to change things. I'm going to make it all better. I've got the computing power now. I've got the programs. I can make any change I want to any event in the past, and I can predict the outcome. I can tell if I step on a bug whether I'm going to change the course of evolution. I can tell if I stop a war whether it's going to make any difference whatsoever. So if I can, why not?'

'Why not? Well, for a start, since when did you get the right to decide, and for seconds, how come you want to get rid of these two?' Again Franklin indicated Jules and Gen.

'Ahh. Well, they are somewhat central to some events in the future. Events that would be better if they never happened.'

'What events?' asked Gen, sparking up as her papaya and ginger juice took effect.

Quincy smiled. 'Well, I can't tell you. Rule 1 still holds, you know, until I decide to change things!'

'So you'll kill kids, you'll change history, just to get what you want?'

'Yip! I will,' said Quincy, suddenly angry. He was just as suddenly calm again. 'Not to get what I want, Franklin. To get what's good for us. For us now. There is only Now, you know. The Past is Gone, the Future's Unknown, the Present Never Happens. Only Now. And only Now matters.'

'You'd destroy the past to make it better Now?'

'Yip! Wouldn't you, wouldn't anyone? Isn't that what survival is ultimately about? Of course you kill what threatens you. The past threatens us, by holding us back. We can change it, we can make things better for us. We should do it.'

Quincy was fired up now, impassioned like he'd been backstage at the launch with Theo.

'And killing kids by sending them to die in Pompeii, that's just part of the plan?'

'Small part, but yip, it is.' Quincy laughed. 'Franklin, when are you going to learn that no one cares? People die all the time, bad stuff happens, who cares? People only care about themselves. Give 'em what they want, they're happy.'

He shook his head and chuckled. 'Ahh, Franklin. You see what I mean about your small vision? I mean, even when you take me on, what do you do? Turn up with a bunch of kids and force me to confess. Pathetic. What are you going to do now? Go out on the street and yell?' Quincy thought this was highly amusing. 'I can see it! Mad-looking Franklin standing in the middle of Metro One yelling at everyone! "Quincy's a bad man. He's trying to take over the world! Put that pizza down!"'

He walked over and slapped Franklin on the shoulder. 'Is that what you're going to do now, Franklin? Is that how you're going to tell the world what an evil, bad man I am?'

Franklin shook his head. 'Nip, nip, that's not what I had in mind, Quince,' said Franklin, reaching out and slapping Quincy on the shoulder in return. 'What I thought we might do was beam our little chat here out live on the *Hurrah*

Banter Show. That way everyone can see it and make up their own mind.'

Quincy stopped chuckling. He looked at Franklin to see if he was serious. 'We've been live? On the ClickDowns?'

Franklin nodded.

'Zif! You couldn't organise that. Hurrah wouldn't have you on.'

'Really?' Franklin spoke into his Coat. 'Honeydew, you've been getting the signal?'

'Loud and clear.' Honeydew's voice was being broadcast by Franklin's Coat. 'Ratings climbing 7.2 every 4.8 seconds. We could be getting more over fifty-fives on Mars, but it's early afternoon there and so a lot of them are at work. Hurrah's loving it, by the way. Wants to know if you'll come on tomorrow. Exclusive!'

Quincy looked around at them all. 'Oh, very good bluff! Bravo! ClickDown!' he ordered at the Wall, and a screen appeared. It showed a wide shot of them all standing in Quincy's gallery. In the corner was a box with a shot of Hurrah. She waved down the camera at Quincy. Along the bottom of the screen scrolled a message: 'This program brought to you by TimeMaster – We Make Time for You.'

Quincy spun round to face them. 'I ... I ... well, how did you ...?'

It was Franklin's turn to chuckle. 'I can't believe you fell for it,' he said. 'I just walked on in, Coat on, beaming out everything, and you just chatted away. I wasn't even sure you'd let us in.'

'But ... but ... it won't matter. Everyone thinks you're mad. They won't care.'

'Really? You know, one day you should Jump to one of the ancient Greek Sites and get them to explain the idea of Hubris to you.'

Quincy looked around at them all. 'You're pathetic. I offer you the chance to grow! To take control, to take the next step in being human. We could truly control our own destiny. And what do you all choose? You choose to stumble on, handcuffed to history, dragging the dead weight of the past with you. Well, you can do it without me.' And Quincy took a step back and vanished.

'Damn!' said Franklin. 'I was hoping he wouldn't Jump.'

'But he got away!' protested Gen. 'We should've stopped him. What are we going to do now? Who knows what he might do?'

'I wouldn't worry about it,' said Franklin. 'He'll have gone somewhere where he thinks he can control everything, but he's finished here. And we'll find him. It might take a bit longer than it did to find Gen, but I think we can figure it out.'

Hurrah cut in. 'Franklin, great show. The kids were terrific. I want everyone on the program tomorrow, Oak Eye? I'll leave Honeydew to organise the details. Talk to you.' She clicked out.

'Hip! That's great,' said Theo. 'We'll get you on Hurrah, do some shots, we can all be famous together!'

'No thanks,' said Gen.

Theo looked at her, surprised.

'Can I just go?' she said. 'I just want to go back home. It's been amazing but, I mean, a lot's happened and I'm just over it all right now, OK?' Gen looked completely strung out.

Jules was feeling a bit the same. This day seemed to have way too many hours in it. He went and stood next to her. 'Me too,' he said. 'You do it, Theo. This is your Now. You be famous. I want to go back to our Now. And just be ... us, I suppose.'

Sonja, Kyeela and Bonnie obviously thought Jules and Gen were insane, but reluctantly they agreed. It was time to return to Mil 3.

Franklin turned to Jules. 'You did an extraordinary thing today.'

Jules blushed and didn't know where to look.

'Yip, it was totally boid,' said Theo, coming over and punching him on the arm. 'I'll try to not think of you as Dodoboy ever again.' He held a hand out to Gen. 'So, kidnapper,' he said, smiling. 'I'm sorry about all that. And about Pompeii and everything. I don't know if we'll see you again ...'

'Don't say that!' said Gen. 'You can drop in, can't you? Franklin? Can't you come and visit once in a while?'

Franklin for once was quiet. He just smiled a small sad smile.

'We're not going to see you again?' asked Gen, distraught.

'Rule 1,' said Franklin quietly. 'And Rule 2, really.'

'There's a Rule 2?' asked Jules.

'Yip,' said Theo. 'Rule 1 is simple. Don't Touch Anything. But then you get a lot of details and explanations. Rule 2 is really simple. It just says, "Don't Even Think About It." That was Quincy's mistake. He didn't think about anything else.'

Gen looked like she was about to cry again.

'This is too hard. After everything ...'

Franklin stepped in. 'Hey, Genevieve,' he said quietly. 'The Future's Unknown. We might see you again. Who knows?'

Gen sniffed a bit, and then nodded. 'OK.'

She took a step forward and hugged Theo. Then she hugged Franklin. Then she stepped back with the girls and Jules.

'I guess we're ready. Bye.'

'Soneehaha,' called out Franklin.

'Flip ya,' said Theo.

They closed their eyes.

Jules felt Gen's hot breath on his cheek.

He pulled away.

It was night time. He looked down at his watch. It was a little before eleven o'clock. He was on the front porch of Gen's house.

Gen hadn't pulled away.

'Thanks for saving me,' she said quietly.

~ *Do you know what to do?* asked his brain.

~ *I think so,* said Jules.

He leant forward, tilting his nose just a little to the left.

His lips brushed against hers.

The door opened. 'Well, hello,' said a perfectly normal-sounding Katherine Corrigan. From upstairs, Jules heard a slight wail of annoyance. Sounded like Cynthia, he thought.

'Look at you two, home on time and everything. Did you have a good night?'

'Yes,' said Jules cautiously.

Katherine smiled happily and Gen's dad came up behind her.

'Hi, kids,' he said, obviously relieved that they were home on time. 'Good movie?'

'Umm?' said Jules. Why could he never remember what film they'd been to see?

~ *Well, it's now three days ago,* reasoned his brain.

~ *No it's not, we're back here. It's Friday night. The movie finished an hour ago.*

~ *Plus three days.*

~ *No, we get to do those three days again, as if nothing had happened. Which it did, but now it's not going to.*

~ *That'll do. Just let me sort that out, OK?*

'Yeah it was great,' said Gen while Jules was bringing his brain up to speed. 'Well, good night, Jules. Thanks again. I had a really nice time.' She ducked forward quickly and gave him a little peck on the check – a little more warmly than she might peck a distant cousin, but a lot less than Jules as boyfriend and daring rescuer might have hoped for.

She went inside, then flashed a dazzling smile back at him, which instantly restored his hopes and dreams.

The door closed.

Once again he wandered back up the road to his own home, lost in thought and reflection on everything they'd seen and experienced that they were now about to not experience.

As he put his key into the door, his father opened it.

'Oh it's you,' Tony Santorini said. 'I thought it was you about five minutes ago, but it was just some guy delivering pizza. He had the address right, but he kept saying it was for Carter. You know anyone called Carter? Anyway, I took it. I thought you might like some. You hungry, you want some pizza?'

His father was offering him pizza? Not wholemeal, stone-ground, wood-fired organic tomato pizza with no pepperoni, but just ordinary home-delivered pizza of the worst possible kind?

Things were looking up.

epilogue

It was Sunday afternoon and Jules was having the weekend he would have had if he had not had the weekend he'd already had.

So he wasn't trying to contact Gen to talk about TimeJumping on Friday night, because they hadn't TimeJumped on Friday night. He wasn't not sleeping, and he wasn't a nervous wreck.

His father was trying to tell him about his mother and couldn't, but Jules wasn't all that worried because he knew what he was trying to tell him. And he remembered, as he would have, about the rehearsal on Monday with Stevie's band. So he was listening to the tape, and trying some things on his keyboard when the doorbell rang.

He leapt up and went to answer it. Gen was walking away as he opened the door. 'Nice of you to answer the door,' she said.

'Sorry. I was listening to something. Come in.'

Inside they flopped down opposite each other on the couches in the lounge room.

Gen pulled out a book from her bag and handed it to Jules. 'Take a look at this.'

Jules looked at the cover: '*The Houses of Pompeii*'.

Gen came and sat down next to him. 'I couldn't look at it on my own. I wanted you to . . . I knew you'd understand. I don't know what I would do if I found something in there.'

Jules turned a page. Was that the street they'd landed in? It looked familiar, the rough stones in the middle of it, the cart-wheel ruts, the houses right on the road. Had they come around that corner? And there was the mountain. It looked so mild compared to when they'd been there.

He turned some more pages. And then stopped.

It was a photo of white figures. All were lying down, some had their hands over their heads. One was protecting a girl, perhaps about Lavinia's age.

Jules read quietly. 'House of Petronius. Perhaps with members of his family and household. Plaster casts of body cavities found in the ruins – Is that Lavinia's family?'

'I don't know. It could be.' Gen was crying. 'Why

couldn't we change that?' she howled. 'Just because Quincy was going to do it all for the wrong reasons, what's wrong with doing it for the right reasons? We could tell them. Get them into boats and rescue them. What's wrong with that?'

'We couldn't,' said Jules. 'You can't change what happens.'

'Really?' asked Gen, standing up and brushing away her tears angrily. 'What about us?' she demanded.

'Us?' said Jules.

'Yeah, us. Are we meant to be visited by some kid from the future and know all about JumpMans, and Fifteen Billion and Seventy-three and all the rest of it? Is that what's meant to happen? Because if it's not, then we're changing history all the time. You know, instead of just being kids growing and going to school, we're kids who know about TimeJumping. Is that what's meant to happen?'

~ *She's got a point,* said his brain.

~ *I know she's got a point. Why didn't you think of that?*

~ *I did. But then you have to think of it as well.*

Jules leant forward on the couch, frowning a little. 'Well, maybe it is all meant to happen.'

'Why?'

'I don't know why, Gen. I don't know why anything happens. But all this stuff, all this TimeJumping, keeps on happening to us. Maybe it's meant to happen.'

Gen snorted, sounding a little like Franklin. 'Jules – it doesn't make any sense. Why us? And anyway, even though it happens to us, now we're going through this weekend again and it's not happening to us. So which is it – are we kids who TimeJumped to Pompeii, or are we kids who went to the movies and came home again? I'd really like to know.'

'I think we're both,' said Jules. And without consulting his brain, or thinking much about it at all, he got up from the couch and went over and put his arm around Gen and hugged her.

Gen sniffed and pressed her head against his shoulder. 'Thanks, Jules,' she said quietly. 'You're a really nice guy.'

Things were *definitely* looking up.

THE GREEDY LITTLE BOY WHO NEVER WAS

A fairytale from Fifteen Billion and Seventy-three, a time three thousand years in the future, where they date everything from the Big Bang, which by current calculations was about fifteen billion years ago, if indeed it happened at all. In this future time, time travel or TimeJumping is as common as a phone call. Kids have their own JumpMans, which allow them to travel to any time they like. And just as we have fairytales to warn us not to go into the woods and start chewing on gingerbread cottages or to keep us wary of any home we might come across where porridge might be cooling on the table, so do the children of this future time have tales to warn them of the dire and unalterable consequences of messing about with history ...

Once upon several times, today, tomorrow and any number of yesterdays you might care to count, there lived a greedy little boy. Let's call him Marvin, because that's what everyone else called him. Marvin wanted what everyone else had. In fact Marvin only really wanted it if someone else had it. He'd throw away his own cake to snatch at someone else's crust of bread. He'd stomp over his own perfect toys to seize a rusty little car much loved by a tearful tot in a sandpit. He'd tear at the hair of girls for their dolls, he'd pummel the arms of boys for their bats and balls, he'd scream down the playground until he had all the kids' bikes and kites and trucks and trikes. Marvin wanted it all and he wanted it now.

Marvin's parents were worn out. Marvin had always been like this. Even as a baby he'd been greedy. He'd screamed for blankets keeping other babies warm, for rattles making other babies laugh, for teddies being hugged in other cots by other toddlers. Whatever it was, he'd want his and everyone else's. He'd thrash around furiously until he could get his little friends' cheese sticks. And their cups. And their rusks. And, well, pretty much everything, until his little friends were hungry and cold and stopped coming around.

Marvin's parents hadn't slept in years. Their hair was grey, their skin a bad yellow, their teeth soft, and they were shorter than they used to be before Marvin was born. When Marvin's dad was at work – he was a pilot on the Mars Shuttle – he used to say, 'I love my boy. He's just a little hard ... to *like*.'

When Marvin's mum was at her work – she was a HyperGardener at Two Planet TerraForm – she used to say, 'I love my boy. It's just ... at times ... I wish ...' and then she would trail off and her friends would nod understandingly. They'd all long ago stopped letting their kids play with Marvin, and whenever it got to his birthday and the invitations went out, somehow everyone was always busy.

To protect Marvin from this, his mum and dad were always organising incredible birthday parties that involved travel or going to shows or a lavish dinner with just the three of them. Nothing that ever involved any other kids.

And so Marvin grew into a boy who got everything he wanted and then a whole lot of other stuff in case it turned out he wanted that as well. It was just easier to get it in the first place. He had no friends, but he didn't really notice that because he was so busy getting other kids' stuff that he didn't care that they didn't like him or want to play with him. And when he went home from school, there was always more stuff at home than he could ever possibly play with, ride on, look at, build, paint, break, or generally use in the time available between stuffing his face and going off to bed. Because of course, he was a greedy little boy when it came to food. He had to have a snack before dinner, two desserts, some snacks before going to bed, a little something on his bedside table in case he got hungry during the night, something to nibble on his way downstairs to breakfast, and so on throughout the day.

Marvin's mum used to like to breed pet armadillos but she was so busy shopping and cooking for Marvin that there was now only Old Tex, an ancient armadillo who didn't do much else but curl up in the corner and snore. Marvin's dad used to love to Solar Blade, and in fact had been close to Region Champion in his youth, but he was now so busy scouring Earth and Mars for things Marvin might like his Solar Blades had gone dark and were last seen hovering somewhere under the roof of the garage.

And so the day came when Marvin was finally old enough to be allowed to join Junior Jumpers, the first stage of learning to TimeJump. Junior Jumpers used special JumpMans to go on short hops, just so they could get the hang of what it meant to visit another time. After a few introductory lessons, they might start by Jumping to five minutes ago. All the kids loved that. It was so funny to see yourself so eager to learn all about TimeJumping and now here you were doing it and watching yourself be so eager to learn all about it. They'd go around and around in that loop for ages!

After a month or two more, during which they'd continue to get the feel of being in the past by Jumping to the day before yesterday or to their last birthday, the night would come when they'd go on their first real TimeJump into real History. Nothing too scary – not like the older kids, who loved to go and see the Asteroid that Killed the Dinosaurs Entering Earth's Atmosphere or The Six Pirates of the Ivory Coast – just something easygoing and fun.

They'd take their Junior JumpMans, check the co-ordinates, point their bright red remotes at the hovering spheres, close their eyes and the next moment they were in – the Desert Sands of Egypt and the Pyramids were rising before their very eyes.

Well, it was fantastic, and every kid sat there silent and invisible and in awe of where they were and how they'd got there. Thousands toiled around them, dragging quarried blocks of rock into place and marching supplies of mortar and food up to the sweating workers, and our Junior Jumpers were in the middle of it all. They'd stay five minutes and then return to their own time, seven or eight thousand years in the future, and do a project on what they'd seen.

Not Marvin.

Throughout Junior Jumpers, he'd been the first kid the JumpMasters wanted to suspend. He'd wanted more Time. He'd gone to back to his own last year's birthday and tried to steal cake from himself. They despaired. But good natured as they were they thought they'd give him one last chance, and off they sent him on the Pyramid Jump.

Bad move.

For Marvin.

They hadn't been there one minute when Marvin darted out of the group and grabbed a tiny toy cow made of clay that a boy had been playing with in the sand while his mother made flour cakes for the workers.

When the JumpMasters tried to make him put it back, he started howling. He howled like a wounded wolf, and across the valley, work stopped. The great rollers ground to a halt as teams of men pushing great blocks of stone up ramps paused, puzzled at this noise coming out of the dunes. For when you

Jump you arrive just a little behind local time and so you're invisible to those operating in the present that you are visiting. As far as the local Egyptians knew there was no one there. So they began to be frightened by Marvin's wail.

The JumpMasters had no choice. Dire historical consequences were looming. They Jumped the group home.

All except Marvin.

He never arrived.

Or, to put it more accurately, he never went.

TimeJumping is only possible if we only go and look. You can't go back and touch anything. Start moving stuff around and who knows what part of history you might change. You could prevent Shakespeare's parents from meeting. You could stop the invention of the wheel, the discovery of fire, or keep us believing the world is flat for centuries longer than we should have.

But Marvin picked up a toy cow.

He picked up the toy cow of his great-great-great-great-great-great-great-great – well, as many greats as you might care to count, really – grandfather. Or rather, someone who would have been his grandfather if he hadn't got into trouble when he went home without his toy cow. And was sent to lie on his reed mat without any dinner. And caught a nasty cold during the night as he lay shivering and hungry. And died the next day.

And so Marvin was never born.

When they Jumped back to Junior Jumper Hall, all heard the smash of the brittle toy cow on the floor. It fell where Marvin would have been if he'd ever existed.

With one greedy grasp he'd unborn himself and no one remembered that he'd ever been. History had become Marvinless.

They puzzled over the broken toy cow for a while, but then they put the pieces up on a shelf and next year's Junior Jumpers were told to be more careful and not to pick things up, and after a few years no one could even remember where it came from in the first place.

And no one ever remembered Marvin, either, the Greedy Little Boy Who Never Was.

James Valentine

James Valentine is a broadcaster on ABC Radio. He is also a reporter for *Showtime Movie News*.

James has been a television presenter and a freelance writer for magazines and newspapers. For many years he was a full-time musician, most notably with Australian band The Models.

James has two young children, Ruby and Roy, and lives in Sydney with his wife, Joanne, a clinical psychologist.